14094

£1.25

£1.25

THE WOOD BEYOND
THE WORLD
BY WILLIAM MORRIS

THE WOOD BEYOND
THE WORLD
BY WILLIAM MORRIS

INTRODUCTION BY TOM SHIPPEY

OXFORD UNIVERSITY PRESS 1980

Oxford University Press, Walton Street, Oxford OX2 6DP

London Glasgow New York Toronto
Delhi Bombay Calcutta Madras Karachi
Kuala Lumpur Singapore Hong Kong Tokyo
Nairobi Dar es Salaam Cape Town
Melbourne Wellington
and associate companies in
Beirut Berlin Ibadan Mexico City

The Wood Beyond the World *was first published by*
the Kelmscott Press, Hammersmith 1894
This edition first published as an Oxford University Press
paperback 1980

Introduction © T. A. Shippey 1980

British Library Cataloguing in Publication Data

Morris, William, b. 1834
The wood beyond the world.
I. Title
823'.8   PR5079.W/   79-41626
ISBN 0-19-281301-3

Printed in Great Britain by
Hazell Watson & Viney Ltd,
Aylesbury, Bucks

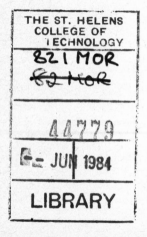

INTRODUCTION

William Morris's last decade has long been a dis
appointment to his biographers. He had developed
well enough in the preceding thirty years or so, living
down the disgrace of a rich father who made his
money from sweated labour in a Devon coppermine,
pursuing simultaneous careers as poet, artist, designer,
weaver, glazier, and much else, eventually 'coming
out' as a Socialist at a time when to be one could
entail some considerable dangers – though not so
much if you were a rich man and a rich man's son.
Morris even went so far as to associate, if not exactly
hobnob, with Karl Marx's daughter Eleanor and
with Friedrich Engels, coauthor of the Communist
Manifesto. But this good middle and bad beginning
did not make for a good end. In 1884 Morris and some
of his friends provoked a split in the 'Social Demo
cratic Federation', leaving it to start their own 'Socialist
League'. This latter organization continued for some
five or six years, till, as Bernard Shaw commented,
the author of its plan for 'AntiState Communism'
discovered, 'after spending a good deal of Morris's
money . . . that the logic of their plan involved the
repudiation of Morris's directorship (and money)
which was keeping the whole affair together. So
Morris, who had been holding the League up by the
scruff of its neck, opened his hand, whereupon it
dropped like a stone into the sea, leaving only a little
wreckage to come to the surface occasionally, a
demand for bail at the police court or a small loan.'
Morris did not change his beliefs, but he gave up

trying to organize political activities. He spent most of his last years publishing books of an inordinately magnificent, expensive and hand-crafted kind through his own Kelmscott Press, and in writing fantasies. Some of these were still decently Utopian or even revolutionary – *A Dream of John Ball*, 1886–7, and *News from Nowhere*, 1890 – but seven were set in places and times so remote that no connection with the real world of politics could ever be made out. Even their titles sound self-indulgent: *The House of the Wolfings, The Roots of the Mountains, The Story of the Glittering Plain* in a relatively 'heroic' group, 1888–90, then in more romantic style from 1894 on *The Wood beyond the World, The Well at the World's End, The Water of the Wondrous Isles, The Sundering Flood*. The last was completed less than a month before Morris's death on 3 October 1896. Though his career has been described as 'romantic to revolutionary', it sounds as if the 'romantic' had the last word after all.

Earnest scholars have accordingly not been kind to these late works, though they have tried to be forgiving. 'Compensation' is the most common excuse offered. Morris was disillusioned by the collapse of the Socialist League, even more so by his unhappy thirty-year-old marriage to Jane Burden. So, the theory goes, he created these 'diffuse' and 'flimsy' books, full of 'compliant, white-armed maidens', as day-dreams, as protections, as a kind of therapy, as a means of hiding from himself the 'basic confusions in his thought' (like being a rich Socialist) which he could not cope with in reality. The keynote of such explanations is Duty. Morris's biographers, armed with hindsight and twentieth-century liberal opinions, feel they know how he should have reacted. Inquiry, apology, gentle rebuke, are therefore implicit in their approaches to much of his writing: he should have known better. But to this view there is one sharp and countervailing image, which is that of Morris in his role as Treasurer of the Socialist League, presiding over a meeting of staggering dullness. The air is thick with points of order from self-important nobodies, the debate shows every sign of protracting itself into eternity from sheer love of disputation. Through it all comes the voice of Morris. 'Mr Chairman, *can't* we get on with the business? I want my TEA!' Wanting one's tea is admittedly rather a Bilbo Baggins reaction ('baggins' is indeed the old Northern English word for 'tea'), but at least there is no doubt about its truth or its immediacy – one might even say its realism. The great mystery of the twentieth century, as George Orwell pointed out in *Coming Up for Air*, is how people have allowed themselves to be distracted from primary gratifications by a grey *apparatchik* utilitarianism, which by further irony often doesn't even work. Morris *could* have kept on writing pompous ephemera like 'The manifesto of the Socialist League, signed by the provisional council at the foundation of the League on 30th December 1884, and adopted at the general conference held at Farringdon Hall, London, on July 5th 1885'. But he wrote *The Wood beyond the World* instead. Even by utilitarian standards, this decision was not self-evidently wrong.

These last seven books by Morris are usually called 'romances' or 'fantasies', in deference to their non-novelistic nature. It is worth considering for a moment whether they could not be called 'historical fictions'.

It is true that not one of them contains a date or an identifiable place-name. Still, they are not completely contextless. The first group of three, from *The House of the Wolfings* to *The Story of the Glittering Plain*, are all set in pagan times among Germanic peoples, Goths or Norsemen. They contain names like 'Mirkwood' and 'the Acre of the Undying', evident translations of Old Norse *Myrkvithr, Ódáinsakr*, and carrying with them faint suggestions of the saga- or edda-worlds from which these names come. The stories are accordingly fierce, contentious, a little gloomy. By contrast the four later works, beginning with *The Well at the World's End* (started before *The Wood beyond the World* but not published till after it, in 1895), are set in Christian epochs, if still in the North-West of Europe; they carry the more mysterious and less morally black-and-white tone of medieval romance. The claim to being 'historical fiction' rests, however, not on the scraps of information dropped here and there inside the stories, but on the notion that they contain what Georg Lukács calls the distinctive feature of the true historical novel, 'derivation of the individuality of characters from the historical peculiarity of their age'. In these books Morris is presenting individual people and destinies. But he is also using them, sometimes more, sometimes less, to suggest the charm and power of past ages.

Most modern historical novelists, attempting that feat, cannot resist the temptation to use the 'Connecticut Yankee at the Court of King Arthur' motif, in other words to introduce some modern character or character with anachronistically modern opinions, to point the difference between then and now: so we have Captain Horatio Hornblower, with his physical squeamishness and dislike of flogging, T. H. White's Merlin, with his Peter Scott postcards and explanation that he happens to be living backwards in time not forwards, Mary Renault's incipiently democratic Theseus, and many more. Morris does not use that trick. Indeed by his heavy use of archaic words, sentence structures and narrative turns, he seems to want to keep modernity at bay, not to present his heroic or medieval worlds even for flattering comparison with his own time (or ours), but to leave them as they are, beautiful and unreachable. It has been well said by Philip Henderson in his biography, *William Morris: his Life, Work and Friends,* 1967, that Morris's aim in poetry was not vividness but rather 'the cool remoteness of pictures on a frieze or the figures on a faded tapestry' – or, one might add, of paintings like Sir Edward Burne-Jones's 'Love Among the Ruins' on the cover of this book, and his frontispiece to the Kelmscott Press edition of *The Wood beyond the World.* All are sharply-focused, too clear indeed for naturalism, full of minute detail like folds in dress and cracks in walls. At the same time these clear sharp images are set in narrative blanks. They feign to be frameless relics, slipped down through the gap of time which has swallowed so much, and now presented without explanation or apology. Many such fragments were brought to light by the thoroughness of nineteenth-century philology, and often they lie at the kernel of modern romance. A part of the genesis of J. R. R. Tolkien's *Lord of the Rings* is the snatch of song from Edgar in *King Lear,* 'Child Roland to the dark tower came'. Morris's group of heroic fantasies owes a similar debt to 'the pathless Mirkwood' of which so many stories are not quite told in the Norse *Eddas*, his romantic ones to the haunting list of lost tales in the sixteenth-century *Complaynt of Scotlande* – 'the tayl of the v[elle] of the varldis end, the taiyl of the reyde eyttyn vitht the thre heydis, the tail of the thre futtit dog of norrouay'. How Morris must have wished these had survived! In the end he wrote some of the tales for himself.

The *frisson* which one can still get from the unknown, or rather from the bare hint on the edge of the unknown, perhaps explains the most characteristic feature of Morris's last four romances, which is their sense of wavering uncertainty. This is not very common in real medieval romances, and when it does occur there one often thinks that the medieval authors (some of them incurably hard-headed, like Sir Thomas Malory) would have eliminated it if possible. Why was the stroke that Sir Balin struck the most dolorous that ever man struck but one, and why should three king-doms be brought by it into 'grete poverté, miseri and wrecchednesse twelve yere'? Because Balin struck it with the Holy Lance with which Longinus smote Our Lord to the heart, says Malory, and seems to think it sufficient explanation. But to any modern reader – and this includes Morris, for Sir James Frazer had published the first edition of his *Golden Bough* in 1890 – the Dolorous Stroke and the Maimed King are wound round with vague anthropological hints of myth and sacrifice and infertility, so much so that the prosaic medieval reactions seem even more deeply subtle. To us romance and fairy-tale have been sharpened by what Tolkien called 'the elvish hone of antiquity'; the sharp bright colours of their surfaces, like the queen's little daughter 'as white as snow, as red as blood, as black as ebony', hint all the more at depths and shadows. It was this effect that Morris aimed at above all. He did not want literal authenticity, still less Utopian propaganda. He wanted to reproduce for others the sensations which saga and romance had aroused in him. Cultural solidity was one of these. Eeriness, the uncertainty of Sir Percival faced with the Grail procession but ordered to silence, was another.

The Wood beyond the World accordingly thrives on loose ends. For though the ends look loose in the mundane world of physical reality, the stress that falls on them and the way strands suddenly twine round each other imply strongly that they are not loose at all, but appear so only because mortals cannot see them in the right number of dimensions. Why should Golden Walter – a nice young man, 'rather wiser than foolisher than young men are mostly wont' – have the sheer unexplained bad luck to marry a wicked woman, and the sudden desire to go away, and then the further misfortune to lose his father, who has been so strongly urged to conciliation? This all appears to be chance, and no other explanation is offered for it. But in romances 'chance' is a tricky phenomenon. One can only say that while the surface of the first few chapters – a bright and glittering surface packed with suddenly glimpsed heraldic signs – presents Sense and Duty, there is beneath it an undertow of Despair in life and Desire for something else. Walter's father feels the 'Katherine' should be a lucky ship, 'whereas she is under the ward of her who is the saint called upon in the church where thou wert christened, and myself before thee; and thy mother, and my father and mother all lie under the chancel thereof, as thou wottest'. But the wind that fills the sails of the 'Katherine' in chapters IV and V blows dead against church and clan and ancient bones; and Walter is happy, as if the gale came from his own heart, as if some inner compass were guiding him to the vision that has called him three times, from the harbour, from his home, from the city where they told him his father was dead.

Just as in the Middle English poem *Pearl*, where a bereaved parent finds himself in a dream-landscape with his heart suddenly and unreasonably light, our natural reaction is to wonder what can be so strong as to outweigh death and sorrow. We may wonder too whether this new power can be good. Morris's agent for projecting that query is the 'carle', the Robinson Crusoe figure unexplainedly present in the green landscape to which the 'Katherine' is driven, itself ominously reminiscent of Circe. He is another loose end. We never find out what happened to him, where he came from, what he did for the Lady. He does say, though, some half-connected things. He is an inheritor; he killed his predecessor; his predecessor died willingly; the carle regrets the killing now. All this hovers on the edge of allegory. Any medieval friar, we can be sure, would by this time have explained that the carle was Man, his predecessor Jesus, that the inheritance of the killing was Peace, and so on. But nothing like this surfaces in Morris, and indeed that interpretation is ruled out by Walter's question and the carle's answer: 'What came thereof? said Walter.

Evil came of it, said the carle.' Is the whole episode pointless, then? It is certainly redundant in a narrative way. But it has roused the interpretative faculty, like the locked door setting every one of Bluebeard's wives groping for keys. Could the second road out of the green land, the one that does *not* lead to the land of the Bears, the one that the carle took after killing his predecessor – could this be perhaps the road to Paradise, or to Hell, for the carle thinks he may have come back from it without his soul; or as in the ballad 'the road to fair Elfland', where the bitter choice of good and evil is never forced on you at all? Again there is no answer, but thoughts of the Fall of Man, the Earthly Paradise, the Land of the Undying begin to buzz like bees in bonnets.

The literary result is that nothing afterwards can be taken as mere narrative, without further significance; the most minute details demand scrutiny and gain clear focus. Once he is past the waste land Walter comes on a cherry-tree (why cherries?), and starts to eat. As he does so (is it cause and effect?) there comes a 'roaring and braying' which disconcerts Walter so much that he faints (faints?) – and it comes from the dwarf of Walter's magic vision, 'clad in his yellow coat, and grinning up at him from his hideous hairy countenance'. This tiny scene is littered with clues, even though we have not yet been introduced to the mystery. For a start the whole thing sounds very like 'Beauty and the Beast', for in that story it is the picking of a rose which angers the Beast and forces the merchant to hand over his daughter. As in many tales from 'Childe Rowland' to Spenser's Cave of Mammon in *The Faerie Queene*, there is a taboo on the food and drink of Fairyland. But to that one might add the thought that cherries (like roses) are a folk-symbol of virginity, the virginity Walter will not be allowed while he is in the Wood to touch; while the dwarf, with his sadism and gibbering and interest in the white flesh of the Maiden 'underneath its raiment', is an evident image of dangerous sexuality. At the end when Walter kills the dwarf he sees that it 'was girt with a big ungainly sax'. 'Sax' means 'knife'? So dictionaries tell us. However it is noticeable that whatever the sax is, the Maiden will not touch it. And when they bury the dwarf (with precautions to ensure he will not rise again) they bury the sax with him too.

Morris, we can be sure, did not mean to tell a Freudian tale, and in any case Freudian interpretations are no more fully satisfactory, for *The Wood beyond the World*, than the medieval friar style of allegory imagined earlier. What Morris wanted was a shimmer of suggestion, a shimmer not even identifiable as primarily religious or sexual or political or historical. The centre of the story is indeed the magic Wood where all appearance is illusion. This is an ancient motif too, used by Shakespeare in *A Midsummer Night's Dream*, by Milton in *Comus*. Morris's Wood is by contrast almost underpopulated, with only four people in it not counting the dwarf or dwarves. The four however go through a quadrille of eavesdroppings. Walter sees the King's Son and the Lady walking naked in the moonlight; he hears the King's Son browbeating the Maiden; the King's Son overhears the Maiden making assignations with Walter; we do not know what the Lady hears. Characters change from truth to lies in mid-sentence, and the Lady shows both anger and fear which seem genuine at the time but are denied by the Maiden. But then the Maiden is a liar, or anyway she *says* she is. Is the lion in the forest a 'sending'; is the hart (heart?) the Lady hunts a real one; why is she so furious when it gets away? Who, besides, sent the vision and the gale which drew Walter to the Wood in the first place? Answers are not given, or not reliably. One result is Walter's fury and weariness at 'this house of guile and lies', so reminiscent of the tedium he found in ordinary life at the start. Another is the sense of looking on at some eternal struggle between unknown powers or principles – for the Maiden does not know where she comes from nor how she became the Lady's slave, while even after the Lady is dead there are hints that she is not quite dead, not safely dead for good and all.

Over the whole Wood there hangs besides a miasma of sexual desire. Walter lusts for and possesses the Lady. He lusts for but may not deflower the Maiden (not till they get to the city). He cannot even touch her, for the Lady would snuffle out his trace. Nevertheless the Maiden is continually present as something to see, to brush past, to smell – even to whip. The Maiden's iron anklet shows she is a thrall, and many Anglo-Saxon laws incorporate an ominous alternative to a fine, 'if he be a thrall, let them take it out of his hide'. The King's Son knows how the Lady chastises her slave, the dwarf has a relish for her tears, even the Maiden seems not wholly averse to the lash: 'O if then there might be some chastisement for the guilty woman, and not mere sundering!' Biographical criticism could be most unpleasant about this. What needs to be said, though, is that the 'glamour' of the Wood contains a menacing element of frustration in desire, from which Walter and the Maiden flee as soon as its spell is snapped by death.

Are we in a fairy-tale about the non-humans who seek continually to gain souls by marriage with the 'children of Adam'? Or in an allegory about Titania and Bully Bottom and the way that love is blind? Or in a myth about how the White Witch of Winter was killed and the Spring-Maiden in her costume of flowers abducted by the sun-hero Golden Walter? *The Wood beyond the World* contains all these inter-pretations and more (the *Spectator* in 1895 thought it was all about Capital and Labour, though Morris wrote in to say it wasn't). Yet it insists all the time on being 'only a story', producing every now and then a bit of quasi-history or geography like the Starkwall, or Langton on Holm, or the stone-age pastoral Bear-folk who lurk in the hinterland of the world like the Cornish giants of English folk-tale. In a medieval romance one suspects that some hermit would be brought on to explain the whole thing as soul's heal, or the bondage of the flesh dissolved by the grace of the Virgin. In the modern world a rather similar if diametrically opposite belief was put forward by W. B. Yeats, who saw all Morris's later romances as celebrating his own pagan ideals of the Green Tree and the Water of Life (though not yet of mystic gyres). But no single explanation can be true. Truth demands a frame, a context, some assurance of where a work comes from and how it is to be judged. Being a modern man rather than a medieval, Morris did not have to pay even lip-service to any orthodoxy, and could therefore present his fictions to be judged entirely on their own merits. The 'cloud of unknowing' which surrounds *The Wood beyond the World* is the product of art, and so to be enjoyed not dispersed.

It might be thought that such a tenuous literary mode would find no imitators, and certainly 'influence' is in this area more than usually hard to prove. Almost certainly J. R. R. Tolkien remembered *The Roots of the Mountains* when he created Gollum; probably *The Wood beyond the World* was an element in the making of Lothlórien, or better still Fangorn, where also characters wander in a network of lies and glimpses and coincidences presided over by a White Wizard, Gandalf, and his counterfeit Saruman, the shape-changer, the 'dwimmer-crafty', master of eidolons and seemings. However Tolkien could read sagas and romances as well as Morris (indeed rather better), so that when one sees similarity it may not be descent from one to another, but rather descent of both from some centuries-old common source. In the same way, if dates of publication were lost, anyone would say that Fletcher Pratt's fantasy *The Well of the Unicorn* was one of the many Tolkien-successors; but actually it came out in 1948, while *The Lord of the Rings* was still only a manuscript. The map of twentieth-century fantasy is a bit like Morris's enchanted wood, full of overhearings and mistaken identities. Still, there are two things that can be credited to Morris with some surety. One is that he showed the power of medieval and Northern and popular legend to a world which had since the Renaissance been educated away from it, and showed also that this was a living power needing no support from scholarship. The other is that he introduced to fantasy a note of baffled yearning, even of homesickness, which many writers have drawn on since.

This is especially true of science fiction, the form above all others conscious of the brevity of life and the isolation of the contemporary in a waste of time. Morris's epigraph to *The House of the Wolfings*, at the very start of his last romantic period, would do almost as a motto for science fiction as well. Just as a man might look back on a winter night at some house he had once lived in in happiness, says Morris, so we are allowed to fantasise:

> As still the dark road drives us on.
> E'en so the world of men may turn
> At even of some hurried day
> And see the ancient glimmer burn
> Across the waste that has no way . . .

Morris was talking about history, of course, while writers of science fiction look to the future. Still, the 'waste that has no way' has meaning for fantasists of either kind. No one can go back into the past. But the future which science fiction writers look to is of course not *the* future, but *a* future, a future they all know will never exist. All fantasy writers know there is no escape. That is why the best of them build a yearning even into their day-dreams. One catches the note at the end of Jack Vance's stories, like those of the end of time in his *The Dying Earth*, 1950. More recently it has been strongly and truly struck by Avram Davidson, whose *The Enquiries of Doctor Eszterhazy*, 1975, presents an analogue of Sherlock Holmes in the Kingdom of Scythia–Pannonia–Transbalkania, an Austro-Hungarian Empire that never was, very much in the style of Morris's 'Mirk-wood' or 'Upmeads' or 'Utterhay'. Works like these, and like Morris's, are neither modern novels, nor ancient folk-tales, nor medieval romances, but have their own rules and proprieties compounded of many predecessors. Maybe the elixir would have mixed itself without William Morris. Still, Morris's brew appeals to exactly the same taste. Odd as it seems, these consciously archaic works of the 1890s have not dwindled down to 'great-great-grandfather's favourites' anything like as fast as their soberly up-to-date contemporaries.

TOM SHIPPEY

WHILE ago there was a young man dwelling in a great and goodly city by the sea which had to name Langton on Holm. He was but of five and twenty winters, a fair-faced man, yellow-haired, tall and strong; rather wiser than foolisher than young men are mostly wont; a valiant youth, & a kind; not of many words but courteous of speech; no roisterer, nought masterful, but peaceable and knowing how to forbear: in a fray a perilous foe, & a trusty war-fellow. His father, with whom he was dwelling when this tale begins, was a great merchant, richer than a baron of the land, a head-man of the greatest of the Lineages of Langton, and a captain of the Porte: he was of the Lineage of the Goldings, therefore was he called Bartholomew Golden, & his son Golden Walter.

Now ye may well deem that such a youngling as this was looked upon by all as a lucky man without a lack; but there was this flaw in his lot, whereas he had fallen into the toils of love of a woman exceeding fair, and had taken her to wife, she nought unwilling as it seemed. But when they had been wedded some six months he found by manifest tokens, that his fairness was not so much to her but that she must seek to the foulness of one worser than he in all ways; wherefore

I

his rest departed from him, whereas he hated her for her untruth and her hatred of him; yet would the sound of her voice, as she came & went in the house, make his heart beat; and the sight of her stirred desire within him, so that he longed for her to be sweet and kind with him, and deemed that, might it be so, he should forget all the evil gone by. But it was not so; for ever when she saw him, her face changed, and her hatred of him became manifest, and howsoever she were sweet with others, with him she was hard and sour.

SO this went on a while till the chambers of his father's house, yea the very streets of the city, became loathsome to him; and yet he called to mind that the world was wide and he but a young man. So on a day as he sat with his father alone, he spake to him and said: Father, I was on the quays even now, and I looked on the ships that were nigh boun, & thy sign I saw on a tall ship that seemed to me nighest boun. Will it be long ere she sail?

Nay, said his father, that ship, which hight the Katherine, will they warp out of the haven in two days' time. But why askest thou of her?

The shortest word is best, father, said Walter, and this it is, that I would depart in the said ship & see other lands.

Yea and whither, son? said the merchant.

Whither she goeth, said Walter, for I am ill at ease at home, as thou wottest, father.

The merchant held his peace awhile, and looked hard on his son, for there was strong love between them; but at last he said: Well son, maybe it were best for thee; but maybe also we shall not meet again.

2

Yet if we do meet, father, then shalt thou see a new man in me.

Well, said Bartholomew, at least I know on whom to lay the loss of thee, and when thou art gone, for thou shalt have thine own way herein, she shall no longer abide in my house. Nay, but it were for the strife that should arise thenceforth betwixt her kindred and ours, it should go somewhat worse with her than that.

Said Walter: I pray thee shame her not more than needs must be, lest, so doing, thou shame both me and thyself also.

Bartholomew held his peace again for a while; then he said: Goeth she with child, my son?

Walter reddened, and said: I wot not; nor of whom the child may be. Then they both sat silent, till Bartholomew spake, saying: The end of it is, son, that this is Monday, and that thou shalt go abroad in the small hours of Wednesday; and meanwhile I shall look to it that thou go not away empty-handed; the skipper of the Katherine is a good man and true, and knows the seas well; and my servant Robert the Low, who is clerk of the lading, is trustworthy and wise, and as myself in all matters that look towards chaffer. The Katherine is new and stout-builded, & should be lucky, whereas she is under the ward of her who is the saint called upon in the church where thou wert christened, and myself before thee; & thy mother, and my father and mother all lie under the chancel thereof, as thou wottest.

Therewith the elder rose up and went his ways about his business, and there was no more said betwixt him and his son on this matter.

HEN Walter went down to the
Katherine next morning, there was
the skipper Geoffrey, who did him
reverence, and made him all cheer,
and showed him his room aboard
ship, and the plenteous goods which
his father had sent down to the quays already, such
haste as he had made. Walter thanked his father's love
in his heart, but otherwise took little heed to his affairs,
but wore away the time about the haven, gazing list-
lessly on the ships that were making them ready
outward, or unlading, & the mariners and aliens
coming and going: and all these were to him as the
curious images woven on a tapestry.

At last when he had well-nigh come back again to
the Katherine, he saw there a tall ship, which he had
scarce noted before, a ship all-boun, which had her
boats out, and men sitting to the oars thereof ready to
tow her outwards when the hawser should be cast off,
and by seeming her mariners were but abiding for
some one or other to come aboard.

SO Walter stood idly watching the said ship,
and as he looked, lo! folk passing him toward the gangway. These were three; first
came a dwarf, dark-brown of hue & hideous, with
long arms & ears exceeding great and dog-teeth that
stuck out like the fangs of a wild beast. He was clad in
a rich coat of yellow silk, and bare in his hand a
crooked bow, and was girt with a broad sax.

4

AFTER him came a maiden, young by seeming, of scarce twenty summers; fair of face as a flower; grey-eyed, brown-haired, with lips full & red, slim and gentle of body. Simple was her array, of a short and strait green gown, so that on her right ankle was clear to see an iron ring.

LAST of the three was a lady, tall and stately, so radiant of visage & glorious of raiment, that it were hard to say what like she was; for scarce might the eye gaze steady upon her exceeding beauty; yet must every son of Adam who found himself anigh her, lift up his eyes again after he had dropped them, and look again on her, and yet again & yet again. Even so did Walter, and as the three passed by him, it seemed to him as if all the other folk there about had vanished and were nought; nor had he any vision before his eyes of any looking on them, save himself alone. They went over the gangway into the ship, and he saw them go along the deck till they came to the house on the poop, and entered it, and were gone from his sight.

There he stood staring, till little by little the thronging people of the quays came into his eye-shot again; then he saw how the hawser was cast off and the boats fell to tugging the big ship toward the harbour-mouth with hale and how of men. Then the sail fell down from the yard and was sheeted home and filled with the fair wind as the ship's bows ran up on the first green wave outside the haven. Even therewith the shipmen cast abroad a banner, whereon was done in a green field a grim wolf ramping up against a maiden, and so went the ship upon her way.

ALTER stood awhile staring at her empty place where the waves ran into the haven-mouth, and then turned aside and toward the Katherine; and at first he was minded to go ask shipmaster Geoffrey of what he knew concerning the said ship and her alien way-farers; but then it came into his mind, that all this was but an imagination or dream of the day, & that he were best to leave it untold to any. So therewith he went his way from the water-side, and through the streets unto his father's house; but when he was but a little way thence, and the door was before him, him-seemed for a moment of time that he beheld those three coming out down the steps of stone and into the street; to wit the dwarf, the maiden, and the stately lady: but when he stood still to abide their coming, and looked toward them, lo! there was nothing before him save the goodly house of Bartholomew Golden, and three children & a cur dog playing about the steps thereof, & about him were four or five passers-by going about their business. Then was he all confused in his mind, & knew not what to make of it, whether those whom he had seemed to see pass aboard ship were but images of a dream, or children of Adam in very flesh.

OWSOEVER, he entered the house, and found his father in the chamber, and fell to speech with him about their matters; but for all that he loved his father, & worshipped him as a wise & valiant man, yet at that hour he might not hearken the words of his mouth, so much was his mind entangled in the thought of those three, and they were ever before his eyes, as if they had been painted on a table by the best of limners. And of the two women he thought exceeding much, & cast no wyte upon himself for running after the desire of strange women. For he said to himself that he desired not either of the twain; nay, he might not tell which of the twain, the maiden or the stately queen, were clearest to his eyes; but sore he desired to see both of them again, & to know what they were.

SO wore the hours till the Wednesday morning, and it was time that he should bid farewell to his father & get aboard ship; but his father led him down to the quays and on to the Katherine, and there Walter embraced him, not without tears & forebodings; for his heart was full. Then presently the old man went aland; the gangway was unshipped, the hawsers cast off; the oars of the towing boats splashed in the dark water, the sail fell down from the yard, and was sheeted home, & out plunged the Katherine into the misty sea and rolled up the grey slopes, casting abroad her ancient withal, whereon was beaten the token of Bartholomew Golden, to wit a B and a G to the right and the left, & thereabove a cross and a triangle rising from the midst.

WALTER stood on the stern and beheld, yet more with the mind of him than with his eyes; for it all seemed but the double of what the other ship had done; and he thought of it as if the twain were as beads strung on one string & led away by it into the same place, and thence to go in the like order, & so on again and again, and never to draw nigher to each other.

CHAPTER III ⁄ WALTER HEARETH TIDINGS OF THE DEATH OF HIS FATHER

AST sailed the Katherine over the seas, & nought befell to tell of, either to herself or her crew. She came to one cheaping⁄town & then to another, and so on to a third and a fourth; & at each was buying and selling after the manner of chapmen; & Walter not only looked on the doings of his father's folk, but lent a hand, what he might, to help them in all matters, whether it were in seaman's craft, or in chaffer. And the further he went and the longer the time wore, the more he was eased of his old trouble wherein his wife & her treason had to do.

But as for the other trouble, to wit his desire & longing to come up with those three, it yet flickered before him; and though he had not seen them again as one sees people in the streets, and as if he might touch them if he would, yet were their images often before his mind's eye; and yet, as time wore, not so often, nor so troublously; & forsooth both to those about him and to himself, he seemed as a man well healed of his melancholy mood.

OW they left that fourth stead, & sailed over the seas, and came to a fifth, a very great and fair city, which they had made more than seven months from Langton on Holm; and by this time was Walter taking heed & joyance in such things as were toward in that fair city, so far from his kindred, & especially he looked on the fair women there, &

desired them, & loved them; but lightly, as befalleth young men.

Now this was the last country whereto the Katherine was boun; so there they abode some ten months in daily chaffer, and in pleasuring them in beholding all that there was of rare and goodly, & making merry with the merchants and the towns-folk, and the country-folk beyond the gates, and Walter was grown as busy and gay as a strong young man is like to be, & was as one who would fain be of some account amongst his own folk.

But at the end of this while, it befel on a day, as he was leaving his hostel for his booth in the market, & had the door in his hand, there stood before him three mariners in the guise of his own country, and with them was one of clerkly aspect, whom he knew at once for his father's scrivener, Arnold Penstrong by name; and when Walter saw him his heart failed him and he cried out: Arnold, what tidings? Is all well with the folk at Langton?

Said Arnold: Evil tidings are come with me; matters are ill with thy folk; for I may not hide that thy father, Bartholomew Golden, is dead, God rest his soul. AT that word it was to Walter as if all that trouble which but now had sat so light upon him, was once again fresh and heavy, & that his past life of the last few months had never been and it was to him as if he saw his father lying dead on his bed, and heard the folk lamenting about the house. He held his peace a while, and then he said in a voice as of an angry man: What Arnold! and did he die in his bed, or how? For he was neither old nor ailing when we parted.

Said Arnold: Yea, in his bed he died: but first he was some what sword-bitten.

Yea, & how? quoth Walter.

Said Arnold: When thou wert gone, in a few days' wearing, thy father sent thy wife out of his house back to her kindred of the Reddings with no honour, and yet with no such shame as might have been, without blame to us of those who knew the tale of thee and her; which, God-a-mercy, will be pretty much the whole of the city.

Nevertheless, the Reddings took it amiss, & would have a mote with us Goldings to talk of booting. By ill-luck we yea-said that for the saving of the city's peace. But what betid? We met in our Gild-hall, & there befell the talk between us; and in that talk certain words could not be hidden, though they were none too seemly nor too meek. And the said words once spoken drew forth the whetted steel; & there then was the hewing & thrusting! Two of ours were slain outright on the floor, and four of theirs, & many were hurt on either side. Of these was thy father, for as thou mayst well deem, he was nought backward in the fray; but despite his hurts, two in the side and one on the arm, he went home on his own feet, & we deemed that we had come to our above. But well-a-way! it was an evil victory, whereas in ten days he died of his hurts. God have his soul! But now my master, thou mayst well wot that I am not come to tell thee this only, but moreover to bear the word of the kindred, to wit that thou come back with me straight-way in the swift cutter which hath borne me & the tidings; and thou mayst look to it, that though she be swift and light, she is a keel full weatherly.

HEN said Walter: This is a bidding of war. Come back will I, and the Reddings shall wot of my coming. Are ye all-boun?

Yea, said Arnold, we may up anchor this very day, or to-morrow morn at latest. But what aileth thee, master, that thou starest so wild over my shoulder? I pray thee take it not so much to heart! Ever it is the wont of fathers to depart this world before their sons.

UT Walter's visage from wrathful red had become pale, and he pointed up street, and cried out: Look! dost thou see?

See what, master? quoth Arnold.

What! here cometh an ape in gay raiment; belike the beast of some jongleur. Nay, by God's wounds! 'tis a man, though he be exceeding mis-shapen like a very devil. Yea and now there cometh a pretty maid going as if she were of his meney; and lo! here, a most goodly and noble lady! Yea, I see; & doubtless she owneth both the two, and is of the greatest of the folk of this fair city; for on the maiden's ankle I saw an iron ring, which betokeneth thralldom amongst these aliens. But this is strange! for notest thou not how the folk in the street heed not this quaint show; nay not even the stately lady, though she be as lovely as a goddess of the gentiles, and beareth on her gems that would buy Langton twice over; surely they must be overwont to strange and gallant sights.

But now, master, but now!

Yea, what is it? said Walter.

Why, master, they should not yet be gone out of eye-shot, yet gone they are.

What is become of them, are they sunk into the earth? Tush, man! said Walter, looking not on

Arnold, but still staring down the street; they have gone into some house while thine eyes were turned from them a moment.

Nay master, nay, said Arnold, mine eyes were not off them one instant of time. Well, said Walter, somewhat snappishly, they are gone now, and what have we to do to heed such toys, we with all this grief and strife on our hands? Now would I be alone to turn the matter of thine errand over in my mind.

Meantime do thou tell the shipmaster Geoffrey and our other folk of these tidings, and thereafter get thee all ready; and come hither to me before sunrise to-morrow, and I shall be ready for my part; & so sail we back to Langton.

HEREWITH he turned him back into the house, & the others went their ways; but Walter sat alone in his chamber a long while, and pondered these things in his mind. And whiles he made up his mind that he would think no more of the vision of those three, but would fare back to Langton, and enter into the strife with the Reddings & quell them, or die else. But lo, when he was quite steady in this doom, & his heart was lightened thereby, he found that he thought no more of the Reddings and their strife, but as matters that were passed and done with, & that now he was thinking and devising if by any means he might find out in what land dwelt those three. And then again he strove to put that from him, saying that what he had seen was but meet for one brainsick, and a dreamer of dreams. But further-more he thought, Yea, and was Arnold, who this last time had seen the images of those three, a dreamer of waking dreams? for he was nought wonted in such

wise; then thought he: At least I am well content that
he spake to me of their likeness, not I to him; for so I
may tell that there was at least something before my
eyes which grew not out of mine own brain. And yet
again, why should I follow them; and what should I
get by it; & indeed how shall I set about it?

HUS he turned the matter over and over;
& at last seeing that if he grew no fool-
isher over it, he grew no wiser, he
became weary thereof, and bestirred him, & saw to the
trussing up of his goods, & made all ready for his
departure, and so wore the day and slept at nightfall;
and at daybreak comes Arnold to lead him to their
keel, which hight the Bartholomew. He tarried
nought, & with few farewells went aboard ship, &
an hour after they were in the open sea with the ship's
head turned toward Langton on Holm.

CHAPTER IV ⁄ STORM BEFALLS THE BARTHOLOMEW, & SHE IS DRIVEN OFF HER COURSE

OW swift sailed the Bartholomew
for four weeks toward the north-
west with a fair wind, and all was
well with ship and crew. Then the
wind died out on even of a day, so
that the ship scarce made way at all,
though she rolled in a great swell of the sea, so great,
that it seemed to ridge all the main athwart. Moreover
down in the west was a great bank of cloud huddled
up in haze, whereas for twenty days past the sky had

been clear, save for a few bright white clouds flying before the wind. Now the shipmaster, a man right cunning in his craft, looked long on sea & sky, and then turned and bade the mariners take in sail and be right heedful. And when Walter asked him what he looked for, & wherefore he spake not to him thereof, he said surlily: Why should I tell thee what any fool can see without telling, to wit that there is weather to hand?

So they abode what should befall, and Walter went to his room to sleep away the uneasy while, for the night was now fallen; & he knew no more till he was waked up by great hubbub and clamour of the shipmen, and the whipping of ropes, and thunder of flapping sails, and the tossing & weltering of the ship withal. But, being a very stout-hearted young man, he lay still in his room, partly because he was a landsman, and had no mind to tumble about amongst the shipmen and hinder them; and withal he said to himself: What matter whether I go down to the bottom of the sea, or come back to Langton, since either way my life or my death will take away from me the fulfilment of desire? Yet soothly if there hath been a shift of wind, that is not so ill; for then shall we be driven to other lands, and so at the least our home-coming shall be delayed, & other tidings may hap amidst of our tarrying. So let all be as it will.

So in a little while, in spite of the ship's wallowing & the tumult of the wind and waves, he fell asleep again, and woke no more till it was full daylight, and there was the shipmaster standing in the door of his room, the sea-water all streaming from his wet-weather raiment. He said to Walter: Young master, the sele of the day to thee! For by good hap we have gotten into another day. Now I shall tell thee that we have striven to beat, so as not to be driven off our course, but all would not avail, wherefore for these three hours we have been running before the wind; but, fair sir, so big hath been the sea that but for our ship being of the stoutest, and our men all yare, we had all grown exceeding wise concerning the ground of the mid-main. Praise be to St. Nicholas and all Hallows! For though ye shall presently look upon a new sea, and maybe a new land to boot, yet is that better than looking on the ugly things down below.

Is all well with ship and crew then? said Walter.

Yea forsooth, said the shipmaster; verily the Bartholomew is the darling of Oak Woods; come up and look at it, how she is dealing with wind and waves all free from fear.

SO Walter did on his foul-weather raiment, and went up on to the quarter-deck, and there indeed was a change of days; for the sea was dark & tumbling mountain-high, and the white-horses were running down the valleys thereof, & the clouds drave low over all, and bore a scud of rain along with them; and though there was but a rag of sail on her, the ship flew before the wind, rolling a great wash of water from bulwark to bulwark.

Walter stood looking on it all awhile, holding on by a stay-rope, and saying to himself that it was well that they were driving so fast toward new things.

THEN the shipmaster came up to him and clapped him on the shoulder and said: Well, ship-mate, cheer up! and now come below again and eat some meat, and drink a cup with me.

15

So Walter went down and ate and drank, and his heart was lighter than it had been since he had heard of his father's death, & the feud awaiting him at home, which forsooth he had deemed would stay his wanderings a weary while, and therewithal his hopes. But now it seemed as if he needs must wander, would he, would he not; & so it was that even this fed his hope; so sore his heart clung to that desire of his to seek home to those three that seemed to call him unto them.

CHAPTER V ⁄ NOW THEY COME TO A NEW LAND

HREE days they drave before the wind, & on the fourth the clouds lifted, the sun shone out & the offing was clear; the wind had much abated, though it still blew a breeze, & was a head wind for sailing toward the country of Langton. So then the master said that, since they were bewildered, and the wind so ill to deal with, it were best to go still before the wind that they might make some land and get knowledge of their whereabouts from the folk thereof. Withal he said that he deemed the land not to be very far distant.

O did they, and sailed on pleasantly enough, for the weather kept on mending, and the wind fell till it was but a light breeze, yet still foul for Langton.

SO wore three days, and on the eve of the third, the man from the topmast cried out that he saw land ahead; & so did they all before the sun was quite set, though it were but a cloud no bigger than a man's hand.

When night fell they struck not sail, but went forth toward the land fair and softly; for it was early summer, so that the nights were neither long nor dark. **B**UT when it was broad daylight, they opened a land, a long shore of rocks & mountains, & nought else that they could see at first. Nevertheless as day wore & they drew nigher, first they saw how the mountains fell away from the sea, and were behind a long wall of sheer cliff; and coming nigher yet, they beheld a green plain going up after a little in green bents & slopes to the feet of the said cliff-wall. No city nor haven did they see there, not even when they were far nigher to the land; nevertheless whereas they hankered for the peace of the green earth after all the tossing and unrest of the sea, & whereas also they doubted not to find at the least good and fresh water, and belike other bait in the plain under the mountains, they still sailed on not unmerrily; so that by nightfall they cast anchor in five-fathom water hard by the shore.

NEXT morning they found that they were lying a little way off the mouth of a river not right great; so they put out their boats and towed the ship up into the said river, and when they had gone up it for a mile or thereabouts they found the sea water failed, for little was the ebb & flow of the tide on that coast. Then was the river deep and clear, running between smooth grassy land like to meadows.

Also on their left board they saw presently three head of neat cattle going, as if in a meadow of a homestead in their own land, and a few sheep; and thereafter, about a bow-draught from the river, they saw a little house of wood & straw-thatch under a wooded mound, & with orchard trees about it. They wondered little thereat, for they knew no cause why that land should not be builded, though it were in the far outlands. However, they drew their ship up to the bank, thinking that they would at least abide awhile & ask tidings and have some refreshing of the green plain, which was so lovely and pleasant.

BUT while they were busied herein they saw a man come out of the house, and down to the river to meet them; and they soon saw that he was tall & old, long-hoary of hair and beard, & clad mostly in the skins of beasts.

He drew nigh without any fear or mistrust, and coming close to them gave them the sele of the day in a kindly and pleasant voice. The shipmaster greeted him in his turn, and said withal: Old man, art thou the king of this country?

The elder laughed; It hath had none other a long while, said he; and at least there is no other son of Adam here to gainsay.

Thou art alone here then? said the master.

Yea, said the old man, save for the beasts of the field & the wood, and the creeping things, and fowl. Wherefore it is sweet to me to hear your voices. Said the master: Where be the other houses of the town?

The old man laughed. Said he: When I said that I was alone, I mean that I was alone in the land and not only alone in this stead. There is no house save

18

this betwixt the sea & the dwellings of the Bears, over the cliff-wall yonder, yea and a long way over it. Yea, quoth the shipmaster grinning, and be the bears of thy country so manlike, that they dwell in builded houses?

The old man shook his head. Sir, said he, as to their bodily fashion, it is altogether manlike, save that they be one and all higher and bigger than most. For they be bears only in name; they be a nation of half wild men; for I have been told by them that there be many more than that tribe whose folk I have seen, and that they spread wide about behind these mountains from east to west. Now sir, as to their souls and understandings I warrant them not; for miscreants they be, trowing neither in God nor his hallows.

Said the master: Trow they in Mahound then?

Nay, said the elder, I wot not for sure that they have so much as a false God; though I have it from them that they worship a certain woman with mickle worship.

Then spake Walter: Yea, good sir, & how knowest thou that? dost thou deal with them at all?

Said the old man: Whiles some of that folk come hither & have of me what I can spare; a calf or two, or a half-dozen of lambs or hoggets, or a skin of wine or cyder of mine own making: and they give me in return such things as I can use, as skins of hart and bear & other peltries; for now I am old, I can but little of the hunting hereabout. Whiles, also, they bring little lumps of pure copper, and would give me gold also, but it is of little use in this lonely land. Sooth to say, to me they are not masterful or rough-handed; but glad am I that they have been here but of late, and are not like to come again this while; for terrible they are of aspect, and whereas ye be aliens, belike they would not hold their hands from off you; & moreover ye have weapons and other matters which they would covet sorely.

Quoth the master: Since thou dealest with these wild men, will ye not deal with us in chaffer? For whereas we are come from long travel, we hanker after fresh victual, and here aboard are many things which were for thine avail.

Said the old man: All that I have is yours, so that ye do but leave me enough till my next ingathering: of wine and cyder, such as it is, I have plenty for your service; ye may drink it till it is all gone, if ye will: a little corn & meal I have, but not much; yet are ye welcome thereto, since the standing corn in my garth is done blossoming, and I have other meat. Cheeses have I and dried fish; take what ye will thereof. But as to my neat and sheep, if ye have sore need of any, and will have them, I may not say you nay: but I pray you if ye may do without them, not to take my milch-beasts or their engenderers; for, as ye have heard me say, the Bear-folk have been here but of late, and they have had of me all I might spare: but now let me tell you, if ye long after flesh-meat, that there is venison of hart and hind, yea, and of buck and doe, to be had on this plain, and about the little woods at the feet of the rock-wall yonder: neither are they exceeding wild; for since I may not take them, I scare them not, & no other man do they see to hurt them; for the Bear-folk come straight to my house, and fare straight home thence. But I will lead you the nighest way to where the venison is easiest to be gotten. As to the wares in your ship, if ye will give me aught I will take it with a good will; and chiefly if ye have a fair knife or two and a roll of linen cloth, that were a good refreshment to me. But in any case what I have to give is free to you and welcome.

HE shipmaster laughed: Friend, said he, we can thee mickle thanks for all that thou biddest us. And wot well that we be no lifters or sea⁄thieves to take thy livelihood from thee. So to⁄morrow, if thou wilt, we will go with thee and upraise the hunt, & meanwhile we will come aland, & walk on the green grass, and water our ship with thy good fresh water.

So the old carle went back to his house to make them ready what cheer he might, and the shipmen, who were twenty and one, all told, what with the mariners & Arnold and Walter's servants, went ashore, all but two who watched the ship & abode their turn. They went well⁄weaponed, for both the master and Walter deemed wariness wisdom, lest all might not be so good as it seemed. They took of their sail⁄cloths ashore, & tilted them in on the meadow betwixt the house & the ship, and the carle brought them what he had for their avail, of fresh fruits, and cheeses, and milk, and wine, and cyder, and honey, and there they feasted nowise ill, and were right fain.

UT when they had done their meat
and drink the master and the ship⁄
men went about the watering of the
ship, and the others strayed off
along the meadow, so that presently
Walter was left alone with the
carle, & fell to speech with him and said: Father,
meseemeth thou shouldest have some strange tale to
tell, & as yet we have asked thee of nought save meat
for our bellies: now if I ask thee concerning thy life,
and how thou camest hither, & abided here, wilt
thou tell me aught?

HE old man smiled on him and said:
Son, my tale were long to tell; and may⁄
happen concerning much thereof my
memory should fail me; and withal there is grief there⁄
in, which I were loth to awaken: nevertheless if thou
ask, I will answer as I may, & in any case will tell
thee nought save the truth.

AID Walter: Well then, hast thou been
long here?
Yea, said the carle, since I was a young
man, and a stalwarth knight.

Said Walter: This house, didst thou build it, and
raise these garths, and plant orchard and vineyard, and
gather together the neat & the sheep, or did some other
do all this for thee?

Said the carle: I did none of all this; there was one
here before me, and I entered into his inheritance, as

though this were a lordly manor, with a fair castle thereon, and all well stocked and plenished.

Said Walter: Didst thou find thy foregoer alive here?

Yea, said the elder, yet he lived but for a little while after I came to him.

E was silent a while, and then he said: I slew him: even so would he have it, though I bade him a better lot.

Said Walter: Didst thou come hither of thine own will?

May-happen, said the carle; who knoweth? Now have I no will to do either this or that. It is wont that maketh me do, or refrain.

Said Walter: Tell me this; why didst thou slay the man? did he any scathe to thee?

Said the elder: When I slew him, I deemed that he was doing me all scathe: but now I know that it was not so. Thus it was; I would needs go where he had been before, and he stood in the path against me; and I overthrew him, and went on the way I would.

What came thereof? said Walter.

Evil came of it, said the carle.

HEN was Walter silent a while, and the old man spake nothing; but there came a smile in his face that was both sly and somewhat sad. Walter looked on him and said: Was it from hence that thou wouldst go that road?

Yea, said the carle.

Said Walter: And now wilt thou tell me what that road was; whither it went and whereto it led, that thou must needs wend it, though thy first stride were over a dead man?

I will not tell thee, said the carle.

Then they held their peace, both of them, and thereafter got on to other talk of no import.

S O wore the day till night came; and they slept safely, and on the morrow after they had broken their fast, the more part of them set off with the carle to the hunting, and they went, all of them, a three hours' faring towards the foot of the cliffs, which was all grown over with coppice, hazel & thorn, with here & there a big oak or ash-tree; there it was, said the old man, where the venison was most and best.

O F their hunting need nought be said, saving that when the carle had put them on the track of the deer & shown them what to do, he came back again with Walter, who had no great lust for the hunting, & sorely longed to have some more talk with the said carle. He for his part seemed nought loth thereto, and so led Walter to a mound or hillock amidst the clear of the plain, whence all was to be seen save where the wood covered it; but just before where they now lay down there was no wood, save low bushes, betwixt them & the rock-wall; & Walter noted that whereas otherwhere, save in one place whereto their eyes were turned, the cliffs seemed well-nigh or quite sheer, or indeed in some places beetling over, in that said place they fell away from each other on either side; and before this sinking was a slope or scree, that went gently up toward the sinking of the wall. Walter looked long and earnestly at this place, and spake nought, till the carle said: What! thou hast found something before thee to look on. What is it then?

Quoth Walter: Some would say that where yonder slopes run together up towards that sinking in the cliff-wall there will be a pass into the country beyond.

The carle smiled & said: Yea, son; nor, so saying, would they err; for that is the pass into the Bear-country, whereby those huge men come down to chaffer with me.

Yea, said Walter; and therewith he turned him a little, and scanned the rock-wall, & saw how a few miles from that pass it turned somewhat sharply toward the sea, narrowing the plain much there, till it made a bight, the face whereof looked well-nigh north, instead of west, as did the more part of the wall. And in the midst of that northern-looking bight was a dark place which seemed to Walter like a downright shard in the cliff. For the face of the wall was of a bleak grey, and it was but little furrowed.

So then Walter spake: Lo, old friend, there yonder is again a place that meseemeth is a pass; whereunto doth that one lead? And he pointed to it: but the old man did not follow the pointing of his finger, but, looking down on the ground, answered confusedly, & said:

Maybe: I wot not. I deem that it also leadeth into the Bear-country by a round-about road. It leadeth into the far land.

ALTER answered nought: for a strange thought had come uppermost in his mind, that the carle knew far more than he would say of that pass, & that he himself might be led thereby to find the wondrous three. He caught his breath hardly, and his heart knocked against his ribs; but he refrained from speaking for a long while;

but at last he spake in a sharp hard voice, which he scarce knew for his own: Father, tell me, I adjure thee by God and All-hallows, was it through yonder shard that the road lay, when thou must needs make thy first stride over a dead man?

THE old man spake not a while, then he raised his head, & looked Walter full in the eyes, and said in a steady voice: NO, IT WAS NOT. Thereafter they sat looking at each other a while; but at last Walter turned his eyes away, but knew not what they beheld nor where he was, but he was as one in a swoon. For he knew full well that the carle had lied to him, and that he might as well have said aye as no, and told him, that it verily was by that same shard that he had stridden over a dead man. Nevertheless he made as little semblance thereof as he might, and presently came to himself, and fell to talking of other matters, that had nought to do with the adventures of the land. But after a while he spake suddenly, and said: My master, I was thinking of a thing.

Yea, of what? said the carle.

Of this, said Walter; that here in this land be strange adventures toward, and that if we, and I in especial, were to turn our backs on them, and go home with nothing done, it were pity of our lives: for all will be dull and deedless there. I was deeming it were good if we tried the adventure.

What adventure? said the old man, rising up on his elbow & staring sternly on him. Said Walter: The wending yonder pass to the eastward, whereby the huge men come to thee from out of the Bear-country; that we might see what should come thereof.

The carle leaned back again, and smiled & shook

his head, & spake: That adventure were speedily proven: death would come of it, my son.

Yea, & how? said Walter.

The carle said: The big men would take thee, and offer thee up as a blood-offering to that woman, who is their Mawmet. And if ye go all, then shall they do the like with all of you.

Said Walter: Is that sure?

Dead sure, said the carle.

How knowest thou this? said Walter.

I have been there myself, said the carle.

Yea, said Walter, but thou camest away whole.

Art thou sure thereof? said the carle.

Thou art alive yet, old man, said Walter, for I have seen thee eat thy meat, which ghosts use not to do. And he laughed.

But the old man answered soberly: If I escaped, it was by this, that another woman saved me, & not often shall that befall. Nor wholly was I saved; my body escaped forsooth. But where is my soul? Where is my heart, and my life? Young man, I rede thee, try no such adventure; but go home to thy kindred if thou canst.

Moreover, wouldst thou fare alone? The others shall hinder thee.

Said Walter, I am the master; they shall do as I bid them: besides, they will be well pleased to share my goods amongst them if I give them a writing to clear them of all charges which might be brought against them.

Y son! my son! said the carle, I pray thee go not to thy death!

Walter heard him silently, but as if he

were persuaded to refrain; and then the old man fell to, and told him much concerning this Bear-folk & their customs, speaking very freely of them; but Walter's ears were scarce open to this talk: whereas he deemed that he should have nought to do with those wild men; and he durst not ask again concerning the country whereto led the pass on the northward.

CHAPTER VII ⁄ WALTER COMES TO THE SHARD IN THE ROCK-WALL

S they were in converse thus, they heard the hunters blowing on their horns all together; whereon the old man arose, & said: I deem by the blowing that the hunt will be over and done, and that they be blowing on their fellows who have gone scatter-meal about the wood. It is now some five hours after noon, and thy men will be getting back with their venison, & will be fainest of the victuals they have caught; therefore will I hasten on before, and get ready fire and water and other matters for the cooking. Wilt thou come with me, young master, or abide thy men here?

Walter said lightly: I will rest and abide them here; since I cannot fail to see them hence as they go on their ways to thine house. And it may be well that I be at hand to command them and forbid, and put some order amongst them, for rough playmates they be, some of them, and now all heated with the hunting and the joy of the green earth. Thus he spoke, as if nought were toward save supper and bed; but inwardly hope and fear were contending in him, and again his heart beat so hard, that he deemed that the carle must surely hear it. But the old man took him but according to his outward seeming, and nodded his head, & went away quietly toward his house.

WHEN he had been gone a little, Walter rose up heedfully; he had with him a scrip wherein was some cheese and hard-fish, & a little flasket of wine; a short bow he had with him, and a quiver of arrows; & he was girt with a strong & good sword, and a wood-knife withal. He looked to all this gear that it was nought amiss, and then speedily went down off the mound, and when he was come down, he found that it covered him from men coming out of the wood, if he went straight thence to that shard of the rock-wall where was the pass that led southward.

NOW it is no nay that thitherward he turned, and went wisely, lest the carle should make a backward cast, and see him, or lest any straggler of his own folk might happen upon him.

For to say sooth, he deemed that did they wind him, they would be like to let him of his journey. He had noted the bearings of the cliffs nigh the shard, and whereas he could see their heads everywhere except from the depths of the thicket, he was not like to go astray.

HE had made no great way ere he heard the horns blowing all together again in one place, and looking thitherward through the leafy boughs (for he was now amidst of a thicket) he saw his men thronging the mound, & had no doubt therefore that they were blowing on him; but being well under cover he heeded it nought, & lying still a little, saw them go down off the mound and go all of them toward the carle's house, still blowing as they went, but not faring scatter-meal. Wherefore it was clear that they were nought troubled about him.

S O he went on his way to the shard; and there is nothing to say of his journey till he got before it with the last of the clear day, and entered it straightway. It was in sooth a downright breach or cleft in the rock-wall, and there was no hill or bent leading up to it, nothing but a tumble of stones before it, which was somewhat uneasy going, yet needed nought but labour to overcome it, and when he had got over this, and was in the very pass itself, he found it no ill going: forsooth at first it was little worse than a rough road betwixt two great stony slopes, though a little trickle of water ran down amidst of it. So, though it was so nigh nightfall, yet Walter pressed on, yea, and long after the very night was come. For the moon rose wide and bright a little after nightfall. But at last he had gone so long, and was so wearied, that he deemed it nought but wisdom to rest him, and so lay down on a piece of green-sward betwixt the stones, when he had eaten a morsel out of his satchel, and drunk of the water of the stream. There as he lay, if he had any doubt of peril, his weariness soon made it all one to him, for presently he was sleeping as soundly as any man in Langton on Holm.

CHAPTER VIII ⋋ WALTER WENDS THE WASTE

AY was yet young when he awoke: he leapt to his feet, & went down to the stream and drank of its waters, and washed the night off him in a pool thereof, and then set forth on his way again. When he had gone some three hours, the road, which had been going up all the way, but somewhat gently, grew steeper, & the bent on either side lowered, & lowered, till it sank at last altogether, and then was he on a rough mountain-neck with little grass, & no water; save that now & again was a soft place with a flow amidst of it, and such places he must needs fetch a compass about, lest he be mired. He gave himself but little rest, eating what he needs must as he went. The day was bright & calm, so that the sun was never hidden, and he steered by it due south. All that day he went, and found no more change in that huge neck, save that whiles it was more & whiles less steep. A little before nightfall he happened on a shallow pool some twenty yards over; and he deemed it good to rest there, since there was water for his avail, though he might have made somewhat more out of the tail end of the day.

HEN dawn came again he awoke & arose, nor spent much time over his breakfast; but pressed on all he might; and now he said to himself, that whatsoever other peril were athwart his way, he was out of the danger of the chase of his own folk.

ALL this while he had seen no four-footed beast, save now & again a hill-fox, and once some outlandish kind of hare; and of fowl but very few: a crow or two, a long-winged hawk, and twice an eagle high up aloft.

AGAIN, the third night, he slept in the stony wilderness, which still led him up and up. Only toward the end of the day, himseemed that it had been less steep for a long while: otherwise nought was changed, on all sides it was nought but the endless neck, wherefrom nought could be seen, but some other part of itself. This fourth night withal he found no water whereby he might rest, so that he awoke parched, and longing to drink just when the dawn was at its coldest.

BUT on the fifth morrow the ground rose but little, & at last, when he had been going wearily a long while, & now, hard on noon-tide, his thirst grieved him sorely, he came on a spring welling out from under a high rock, the water where-from trickled feebly away. So eager was he to drink, that at first he heeded nought else; but when his thirst was fully quenched his eyes caught sight of the stream which flowed from the well, & he gave a shout, for lo! it was running south. Wherefore it was with a merry heart that he went on, and as he went, came on more streams, all running south or thereabouts. He hastened on all he might, but in despite of all the speed he made, and that he felt the land now going down southward, night overtook him in that same wilder-ness. Yet when he stayed at last for sheer weariness, he lay down in what he deemed by the moonlight to be a shallow valley, with a ridge at the southern end thereof.

E slept long, and when he awoke the sun was high in the heavens, and never was brighter or clearer morning on the earth than was that. He arose and ate of what little was yet left him, and drank of the water of a stream which he had followed the evening before, and beside which he had laid him down; and then set forth again with no great hope to come on new tidings that day. But yet when he was fairly afoot, himseemed that there was something new in the air which he breathed, that was soft and bore sweet scents home to him; whereas heretofore, & that especially for the last three or four days, it had been harsh and void, like the face of the desert itself.

O on he went, and presently was mounting the ridge aforesaid, and, as oft happens when one climbs a steep place, he kept his eyes on the ground, till he felt he was on the top of the ridge. Then he stopped to take breath, & raised his head & looked, and lo! he was verily on the brow of the great mountain-neck, and down below him was the hanging of the great hill-slopes, which fell down, not slowly, as those he had been those days a-mounting, but speedily enough, though with little of broken places or sheer cliffs. But beyond this last of the desert there was before him a lovely land of wooded hills, green plains, and little valleys, stretching out far & wide, till it ended at last in great blue mountains & white snowy peaks beyond them.

HEN for very surprise of joy his spirit wavered, & he felt faint and dizzy, so that he was fain to sit down a while and cover his face with his hands. Presently he came to his sober mind again, and stood up and looked forth keenly, and saw no sign of any dwelling of man. But he said to himself that that might well be because the good & well-grassed land was still so far off, & that he might yet look to find men and their dwellings when he had left the mountain wilderness quite behind him. So therewith he fell to going his ways down the mountain, and lost little time therein, whereas he now had his livelihood to look to.

CHAPTER IX ⁄ WALTER HAPPENETH ON THE FIRST OF THOSE THREE CREATURES

 HAT with one thing, what with another, as his having to turn out of his way for sheer rocks, or for slopes so steep that he might not try the peril of them, & again for bogs impassable, he was fully three days more before he had quite come out of the stony waste, and by that time, though he had never lacked water, his scanty victual was quite done, for all his careful husbandry thereof. But this troubled him little, whereas he looked to find wild fruits here & there, and to shoot some small deer, as hare or coney, and make a shift to cook the same, since he had with him flint and fire-steel. Moreover the further he went, the surer he was that he should soon come across a dwelling, so smooth & fair as everything looked before him. And he had scant fear, save that he might happen on men who should enthrall him.

UT when he was come down past the first green slopes, he was so worn, that he said to himself that rest was better than meat, so little as he had slept for the last three days; so he laid him down under an ash-tree by a stream-side, nor asked what was o-clock, but had his fill of sleep, and even when he awoke in the fresh morning was little fain of rising, but lay betwixt sleeping and waking for some three hours more; then he arose, and went further down the next green bent, yet somewhat slowly because of his hunger-weakness. And the scent of that fair land came up to him like the odour of one great nosegay.

O he came to where the land was level, and there were many trees, as oak and ash, and sweet-chestnut and wych-elm, and hornbeam and quicken-tree, not growing in a close wood or tangled thicket, but set as though in order on the flowery greensward, even as it might be in a great king's park.

So came he to a big bird-cherry, whereof many boughs hung low down laden with fruit: his belly rejoiced at the sight, and he caught hold of a bough, and fell to plucking and eating. But whiles he was amidst of this, he heard suddenly, close anigh him, a strange noise of roaring and braying, not very great, but exceeding fierce and terrible, and not like to the voice of any beast that he knew. As has been aforesaid, Walter was no faint-heart; but what with the weakness of his travail and hunger, what with the strangeness of his adventure and his loneliness, his spirit failed him; he turned round towards the noise, his knees shook & he trembled: this way and that he looked, and then gave a great cry & tumbled down in a swoon; for close before him, at his very feet, was the dwarf whose image he had seen before, clad in his yellow coat, & grinning up at him from his hideous hairy countenance.

OW long he lay there as one dead, he knew not, but when he woke again there was the dwarf sitting on his hams close by him. And when he lifted up his head, the dwarf sent out that fearful harsh voice again; but this time Walter could make out words therein, & knew that the creature spoke and said: How now! What art thou? Whence comest? What wantest?

Walter sat up and said: I am a man; I hight Golden Walter; I come from Langton; I want victual.

Said the dwarf, writhing his face grievously, & laughing forsooth: I know it all: I asked thee to see what wise thou wouldst lie. I was sent forth to look for thee; and I have brought thee loathsome bread with me, such as ye aliens must needs eat: take it!

Therewith he drew a loaf from a satchel which he bore, and thrust it towards Walter, who took it somewhat doubtfully for all his hunger.

The dwarf yelled at him: Art thou dainty, alien? Wouldst thou have flesh? Well, give me thy bow & an arrow or two, since thou art lazy-sick, & I will get thee a coney or a hare, or a quail maybe. Ah, I forgot; thou art dainty, and wilt not eat flesh as I do, blood & all together, but must needs half burn it in the fire, or mar it with hot water; as they say my Lady does: or as the Wretch, the Thing does; I know that, for I have seen It eating.

Nay, said Walter, this sufficeth; & he fell to eating the bread, which was sweet between his teeth. Then when he had eaten a while, for hunger compelled him, he said to the dwarf: But what meanest thou by the Wretch and the Thing? And what Lady is thy Lady?

The creature let out another wordless roar as of furious anger; & then the words came: It hath a face white and red, like to thine; and hands white as thine, yea, but whiter; & the like it is underneath its raiment, only whiter still: for I have seen It . . . yes, I have seen It; ah yes and yes and yes.

And therewith his words ran into gibber and yelling, and he rolled about and smote at the grass: but in a while he grew quiet again and sat still, and then fell to laughing horribly again, & then said: But thou, fool, wilt think It fair if thou fallest into Its hands, and wilt repent it thereafter, as I did. Oh, the mocking and gibes of It, and the tears and shrieks of It; and the knife! What! sayest thou of my Lady? . . . What Lady? O alien, what other Lady is there? And what shall I tell thee of her? it is like that she made me, as she made the Bear men. But she made not the Wretch, the Thing; & she hateth It sorely, as I do. And some day to come . . .

Thereat he brake off and fell to wordless yelling a long while, & thereafter spake all panting: Now I have told thee overmuch, and O if my Lady come to hear thereof. Now I will go.

And therewith he took out two more loaves from his wallet, & tossed them to Walter, and so turned and went his ways; whiles walking upright, as Walter had seen his image on the quay of Langton; whiles bounding and rolling like a ball thrown by a lad; whiles scuttling along on all-fours like an evil beast, and ever and anon giving forth that harsh and evil cry.

Walter sat a while after he was out of sight, so stricken with horror and loathing and a fear of he knew not what, that he might not move. Then he plucked up a heart, and looked to his weapons and put the other loaves into his scrip.

Then he arose and went his ways wondering, yea and dreading, what kind of creature he should next fall in with. For soothly it seemed to him that it would be worse than death if they were all such as this one; and that if it were so, he must needs slay and be slain.

CHAPTER X ⟋ WALTER HAPPENETH ON ANOTHER CREATURE IN THE STRANGE LAND

UT as he went on through the fair and sweet land so bright and sunlitten, and he now rested & fed, the horror & fear ran off from him, and he wandered on merrily, neither did aught befall him save the coming of night, when he laid him down under a great spreading oak with his drawn sword ready to hand, & fell asleep at once, and woke not till the sun was high.

HEN he arose and went on his way again; and the land was no worser than yesterday; but even better, it might be; the greensward more flowery, the oaks & chestnuts greater. Deer of diverse kinds he saw, & might easily have got his meat thereof; but he meddled not with them since he had his bread, & was timorous of lighting a fire. Withal he doubted little of having some entertainment; & that, might be, nought evil; since even that fearful dwarf had been courteous to him after his kind, and had done him good and not harm. But of the happening on the Wretch & the Thing, whereof the dwarf spake, he was yet somewhat afeard.

AFTER he had gone a while and whenas the summer morn was at its brightest, he saw a little way ahead a grey rock rising up from amidst of a ring of oak-trees; so he turned thither straightway; for in this plain land he had seen no rocks heretofore; and as he went he saw that there was a fountain gushing out from under the rock, which ran thence in a fair little stream. And when he had the rock and the fountain and the stream clear before him, lo! a child of Adam sitting beside the fountain under the shadow of the rock. He drew a little nigher, & then he saw that it was a woman, clad in green like the sward whereon she lay. She was playing with the welling out of the water, & she had trussed up her sleeves to the shoulder that she might thrust her bare arms therein. Her shoes of black leather lay on the grass beside her, & her feet and legs yet shone with the brook.

BELIKE amidst the splashing & clatter of the water she did not hear him drawing nigh, so that he was close to her before she lifted up her face & saw him, and he beheld her, that it was the maiden of the thrice-seen pageant. She reddened when

39

she saw him, & hastily covered up her legs with her gown-skirt, & drew down the sleeves over her arms, but otherwise stirred not. As for him, he stood still, striving to speak to her; but no word might he bring out, and his heart beat sorely.

UT the maiden spake to him in a clear sweet voice, wherein was now no trouble: Thou art an alien, art thou not? For I have not seen thee before.

Yea, he said, I am an alien; wilt thou be good to me?

She said: And why not? I was afraid at first, for I thought it had been the King's Son. I looked to see none other; for of goodly men he has been the only one here in the land this long while, till thy coming.

He said: Didst thou look for my coming at about this time?

O nay, she said; how might I?

Said Walter: I wot not; but the other man seemed to be looking for me, and knew of me, and he brought me bread to eat.

She looked on him anxiously, and grew somewhat pale, as she said: What other one?

Now Walter did not know what the dwarf might be to her, fellow-servant or what not, so he would not show his loathing of him; but answered wisely: The little man in the yellow raiment.

UT when she heard that word, she went suddenly very pale, & leaned her head aback, and beat the air with her hands; but said presently in a faint voice: I pray thee talk not of that one while I am by, nor even think of him, if thou mayest forbear.

E spake not, and she was a little while before she came to herself again; then she opened her eyes, & looked upon Walter & smiled kindly on him, as though to ask his pardon for having scared him. Then she rose up in her place, and stood before him; and they were nigh together, for the stream betwixt them was little.

But he still looked anxiously upon her and said: Have I hurt thee? I pray thy pardon.

She looked on him more sweetly still, and said: O nay; thou wouldst not hurt me, thou!

Then she blushed very red, & he in likewise; but afterwards she turned pale, & laid a hand on her breast, & Walter cried out hastily: O me! I have hurt thee again. Wherein have I done amiss?

In nought, in nought, she said; but I am troubled, I wot not wherefore; some thought hath taken hold of me, and I know it not. Mayhappen in a little while I shall know what troubles me. Now I bid thee depart from me a little, and I will abide here; & when thou comest back, it will either be that I have found it out or not; and in either case I will tell thee.

HE spoke earnestly to him; but he said: How long shall I abide away? Her face was troubled as she answered him: For no long while.

E smiled on her and turned away, and went a space to the other side of the oak-trees, whence she was still within eye-shot. There he abode until the time seemed long to him; but he schooled himself and forbore; for he said: Lest she send me away again. So he abided until again the time seemed long to him, & she called not to him: but once again he forbore to go; then at last he arose, and his heart beat and he trembled, and he walked back again speedily, and came to the maiden, who was still standing by the rock of the spring, her arms hanging down, her eyes downcast. She looked up at him as he drew nigh, & her face changed with eagerness as she said: I am glad thou art come back, though it be no long while since thy departure (sooth to say it was scarce half an hour in all). Nevertheless I have been thinking many things, and thereof will I now tell thee.

He said: Maiden, there is a river betwixt us, though it be no big one. Shall I not stride over, and come to thee, that we may sit down together side by side on the green grass?

Nay, she said, not yet; tarry a while till I have told thee of matters. I must now tell thee of my thoughts in order.

Her colour went and came now, and she plaited the folds of her gown with restless fingers. At last she said: Now the first thing is this; that though thou hast seen me first only within this hour, thou hast set thine heart upon me to have me for thy speech-friend and thy darling. And if this be not so, then is all my speech, yea & all my hope, come to an end at once.

O yea! said Walter, even so it is: but how thou hast found this out I wot not; since now for the first time I say it, that thou art indeed my love, and my dear and my darling.

Hush, she said, hush! lest the wood have ears, & thy speech is loud: abide, & I shall tell thee how I know it. Whether this thy love shall outlast the first time that thou holdest my body in thine arms, I wot not, nor dost thou. But sore is my hope that it may be so; for I also, though it be but scarce an hour since I set eyes on thee, have cast mine eyes on thee to have thee for my love and my darling, and my speech-friend. And this is how I wot that thou lovest me, my friend. Now is all this dear & joyful, and over-flows my heart with sweetness. But now must I tell thee of the fear and the evil which lieth behind it.

THEN Walter stretched out his hands to her, & cried out: Yea, yea! But whatever evil entangle us, now we both know these two things, to wit, that thou lovest me, & I thee, wilt thou not come hither, that I may cast mine arms about thee, & kiss thee, if not thy kind lips or thy friendly face at all, yet at least thy dear hand: yea, that I may touch thy body in some wise?

She looked on him steadily, & said softly: Nay, this above all things must not be; and that it may not be is a part of the evil which entangles us. But hearken, friend, once again I tell thee that thy voice is over loud in this wilderness fruitful of evil. Now I have told thee, indeed, of two things whereof we both wot; but next I must needs tell thee of things whereof I wot, and thou wottest not. Yet this were better, that thou pledge thy word not to touch so much as one of my hands, and that we go together a little way hence away from these tumbled stones, & sit down upon the open greensward; whereas here is cover if there be spying abroad.

Again, as she spoke, she turned very pale; but Walter said: Since it must be so, I pledge thee my word to thee as I love thee.

And therewith she knelt down, & did on her

foot-gear, and then sprang lightly over the rivulet; &
then the twain of them went side by side some half a
furlong thence, and sat down, shadowed by the
boughs of a slim quicken-tree growing up out of the
greensward, whereon for a good space around was
neither bush nor brake.

THERE began the maiden to talk soberly,
and said: This is what I must needs say to
thee now, that thou art come into a land
perilous for any one that loveth aught of good; from
which, forsooth, I were fain that thou wert gotten
away safely, even though I should die of longing for
thee. As for myself, my peril is, in a measure, less than
thine; I mean the peril of death. But lo, thou, this iron
on my foot is token that I am a thrall, and thou knowest in what wise thralls must pay for transgressions.
Furthermore, of what I am, and how I came hither,
time would fail me to tell; but somewhile, maybe, I
shall tell thee. I serve an evil mistress, of whom I may
say that scarce I wot if she be a woman or not; but by
some creatures is she accounted for a god, & as a god
is heried; and surely never god was crueller nor colder
than she. Me she hateth sorely; yet if she hated me little
or nought, small were the gain to me if it were her
pleasure to deal hardly by me. But as things now are,
& are like to be, it would not be for her pleasure, but
for her pain and loss, to make an end of me, therefore,
as I said e'en now, my mere life is not in peril with her;
unless, perchance, some sudden passion get the better
of her, and she slay me, and repent of it thereafter.
For so it is, that if it be the least evil of her conditions
that she is wanton, at least wanton she is to the letter.
Many a time hath she cast the net for the catching of

44

some goodly young man; & her latest prey (save it be thou) is the young man whom I named, when first I saw thee, by the name of the King's Son. He is with us yet, and I fear him; for of late hath he wearied of her, though it is but plain truth to say of her, that she is the wonder of all Beauties of the World. He hath wearied of her, I say, and hath cast his eyes upon me, & if I were heedless, he would betray me to the utter/ most of the wrath of my mistress. For needs must I say of him, though he be a goodly man, and now fallen into thralldom, that he hath no bowels of compassion; but is a dastard, who for an hour's pleasure would undo me, and thereafter stand by smiling and taking my mistress's pardon with good cheer, while for me would be no pardon. Seest thou, therefore, how it is with me between these two cruel fools? And moreover there are others of whom I will not even speak to thee.

And therewith she put her hands before her face, and wept, and murmured: Who shall deliver me from this death in life?

But Walter cried out: For what else am I come hither, I, I?

And it was a near thing that he did not take her in his arms, but he remembered his pledged word, and drew aback from her in terror, whereas he had an inkling of why she would not suffer it; & he wept with her.

BUT suddenly the Maid left weeping, and said in a changed voice: friend, whereas thou speakest of delivering me, it is more like that I shall deliver thee. And now I pray thy pardon for thus grieving thee with my grief, and that more especially because thou mayst not solace thy grief with kisses and caresses; but so it was, that for once I was smitten by the thought of the anguish of this land, & the joy of all the world besides.

Therewith she caught her breath in a half-sob, but refrained her & went on: Now dear friend and darling, take good heed to all that I shall say to thee, whereas thou must do after the teaching of my words. And first, I deem by the monster having met thee at the gates of the land, & refreshed thee, that the Mistress hath looked for thy coming; nay, by thy coming hither at all, that she hath cast her net & caught thee. Hast thou noted aught that might seem to make this more like?

Said Walter: Three times in full daylight have I seen go past me the images of the monster and thee and a glorious lady, even as if ye were alive.

And therewith he told her in few words how it had gone with him since that day on the quay at Langton. SHE said: Then it is no longer perhaps, but certain, that thou art her latest catch; and even so I deemed from the first: &, dear friend, this is why I have not suffered thee to kiss or caress me, so sore as I longed for thee. For the Mistress will have thee for her only, and hath lured thee hither for nought else; and she is wise in wizardry (even as some deal am I), & wert thou to touch me with hand or mouth on my naked flesh, yea, or were it even my raiment, then would she scent the savour of thy love upon me, and then, though it may be she would spare thee, she would not spare me.

HEN was she silent a little, and seemed very downcast, & Walter held his peace from grief & confusion & helplessness; for of wizardry he knew nought.

T last the Maid spake again, and said: Nevertheless we will not die redeless. Now thou must look to this, that from hence forward it is thee, & not the King's Son, whom she desireth, & that so much the more that she hath not set eyes on thee. Remember this, whatsoever her seeming may be to thee. Now, therefore, shall the King's Son be free, though he know it not, to cast his love on whomso he will; and, in a way, I also shall be free to yeasay him. Though, forsooth, so fulfilled is she with malice and spite, that even then she may turn round on me to punish me for doing that which she would have me do. Now let me think of it.

HEN was she silent a good while, and spoke at last: Yea, all things are perilous, and a perilous rede I have thought of, whereof I will not tell thee as yet; so waste not the short while by asking me. At least the worst will be no worse than what shall come if we strive not against it. And now, my friend, amongst perils it is growing more and more perilous that we twain should be longer together. But I would say one thing yet; and maybe another thereafter. Thou hast cast thy love upon one who will be true to thee, whatsoever may befall; yet is she a guileful creature, and might not help it her life long, and now for thy very sake must needs be more guileful now than ever before. And as for me, the guileful, my love have I cast upon a lovely man, and one true and simple, and a stout-heart; but at such a pinch is he,

47

that if he withstand all temptation, his withstanding may belike undo both him and me. Therefore swear we both of us, that by both of us shall all guile & all falling away be forgiven on the day when we shall be free to love each the other as our hearts will.

WALTER cried out: O love, I swear it indeed! thou art my Hallow, and I will swear it as on the relics of a Hallow; on thy hands and thy feet I swear it.

The words seemed to her a dear caress; and she laughed, and blushed, and looked full kindly on him; and then her face grew solemn, and she said: On thy life I swear it!

THEN she said: Now is there nought for thee to do but to go hence straight to the Golden House, which is my Mistress's house, and the only house in this land (save one which I may not see), and lieth southward no long way. How she will deal with thee, I wot not; but all I have said of her and thee and the King's Son is true. Therefore I say to thee, be wary and cold at heart, whatsoever outward semblance thou mayst make. If thou have to yield thee to her, then yield rather late than early, so as to gain time. Yet not so late as to seem shamed in yielding for fear's sake. Hold fast to thy life, my friend, for in warding that, thou wardest me from grief without remedy. Thou wilt see me ere long; it may be to-morrow, it may be some days hence. But forget not, that what I may do, that I am doing. Take heed also that thou pay no more heed to me, or rather less, than if thou wert meeting a maiden of no account in the streets of thine own town. O my love! barren is this first farewell, as was our first meeting; but surely shall there be another meeting better than the first, & the last farewell may be long and long yet.

Therewith she stood up, & he knelt before her a little while without any word, & then arose and went his ways; but when he had gone a space he turned about, and saw her still standing in the same place; she stayed a moment when she saw him turn, and then herself turned about.

So he departed through the fair land, and his heart was full with hope & fear as he went.

CHAPTER XI ⁄ WALTER HAPPENETH ON THE MISTRESS

T was but a little after noon when Walter left the Maid behind: he steered south by the sun, as the Maid had bidden him, & went swiftly; for, as a good knight wending to battle, the time seemed long to him till he should meet the foe.

S O an hour before sunset he saw something white & gay gleaming through the boles of the oak⁄trees, & presently there was clear before him a most goodly house builded of white marble, carved all about with knots and imagery, and the carven folk were all painted of their lively colours, whether it were their raiment or their flesh, and the housings wherein they stood all done with gold and fair hues. Gay were the windows of the house; & there was a pillared porch before the great door, with images betwixt the pillars both of men and beasts: and when Walter looked up to the roof of the house, he saw that it gleamed & shone; for all the tiles were of yellow metal, which he deemed to be of very gold.

ALL this he saw as he went, and tarried not to gaze upon it; for he said, belike there will be time for me to look on all this before I die. But he said also, that, though the house was not of the greatest, it was beyond compare of all houses of the world.

NOW he entered it by the porch, & came into a hall many-pillared, & vaulted over, the walls painted with gold and ultramarine, the floor dark, and spangled with many colours, and the windows glazed with knots & pictures. Midmost thereof was a fountain of gold, whence the water ran two ways in gold-lined runnels, spanned twice with little bridges of silver. Long was that hall, and now not very light, so that Walter was come past the fountain before he saw any folk therein: then he looked up toward the high-seat, and him-seemed that a great light shone thence, & dazzled his eyes; & he went on a little way, & then fell on his knees; for there before him on the high-seat sat that wondrous Lady, whose lively image had been shown to him thrice before; and she was clad in gold & jewels, as he had erst seen her. But now she was not alone; for by her side sat a young man, goodly enough, so far as Walter might see him, & most richly clad, with a jewelled sword by his side, & a chaplet of gems on his head. They held each other by the hand, and seemed to be in dear converse together; but they spake softly, so that Walter might not hear what they said, till at last the man spake aloud to the Lady: Seest thou not that there is a man in the hall?

Yea, she said, I see him yonder, kneeling on his knees; let him come nigher & give some account of himself.

So Walter stood up and drew nigh, and stood there, all shamefaced and confused, looking on those twain, & wondering at the beauty of the Lady. As for the man, who was slim, and black-haired, and straight-featured, for all his goodliness Walter accounted him little, & nowise deemed him to look chieftain-like.

OW the Lady spake not to Walter any more than erst; but at last the man said: Why doest thou not kneel as thou didst erewhile?

Walter was on the point of giving him back a fierce answer; but the Lady spake and said: Nay, friend, it matters not whether he kneel or stand; but he may say, if he will, what he would have of me, & wherefore he is come hither.

Then spake Walter, for as wroth & ashamed as he was: Lady, I have strayed into this land, & have come to thine house as I suppose, and if I be not welcome, I may well depart straightway, & seek a way out of thy land, if thou wouldst drive me thence, as well as out of thine house.

Thereat the Lady turned and looked on him, and when her eyes met his, he felt a pang of fear and desire mingled shoot through his heart. This time she spoke to him; but coldly, without either wrath or any thought of him: New-comer, she said, I have not bidden thee hither; but here mayst thou abide a while if thou wilt; nevertheless, take heed that here is no King's Court. There is, forsooth, a folk that serveth me (or, it may be, more than one), of whom thou wert best to know nought. Of others I have but two servants, whom thou wilt see; & the one is a strange creature, who should scare thee or scathe thee with a good will, but of a good will shall serve nought save me; the other is a woman, a thrall, of little avail, save that, being compelled, she will work woman's service for me, but whom none else shall compel . . . Yea, but what is all this to thee; or to me that I should tell it thee? I will not drive thee away; but if thine entertainment please thee not, make no plaint thereof to me, but depart at thy will. Now is this talk betwixt us overlong, since, as thou seest, I & this King's Son are in converse together. Art thou a King's Son?

Nay, Lady, said Walter, I am but of the sons of the merchants.

It matters not, she said; go thy ways into one of the chambers.

And straightway she fell a-talking to the man who sat beside her concerning the singing of the birds beneath her window in the morning; and of how she had bathed her that day in a pool of the woodlands, when she had been heated with hunting, & so forth; and all as if there had been none there save her and the King's Son.

BUT Walter departed all ashamed, as though he had been a poor man thrust away from a rich kinsman's door; & he said to himself that this woman was hateful, and nought love-worthy, & that she was little like to tempt him, despite all the fairness of her body.

N O one else he saw in the house that even: he found meat and drink duly served on a fair table, and thereafter he came on a goodly bed, & all things needful, but no child of Adam to do him service, or bid him welcome or warning. Nevertheless he ate, and drank, and slept, and put off thought of all these things till the morrow, all the more as he hoped to see the kind maiden some time betwixt sunrise and sunset on that new day.

CHAPTER XII ⸝ THE WEARING OF FOUR DAYS IN THE WOOD BEYOND THE WORLD

 E arose betimes, but found no one to greet him, neither was there any sound of folk moving within the fair house; so he but broke his fast, and then went forth and wandered amongst the trees, till he found him a stream to bathe in, and after he had washed the night off him he lay down under a tree thereby for a while, but soon turned back toward the house, lest perchance the Maid should come thither and he should miss her. I T should be said that half a bow⸝shot from the house on that side (i.e. due north thereof) was a little hazel⸝brake, and round about it the trees were smaller of kind than the oaks and chestnuts he had passed through before, being mostly of birch & quicken⸝beam and young ash, with small wood betwixt them; so now he passed through the thicket, and, coming to the edge thereof, beheld the Lady and

the King's Son walking together hand in hand, full lovingly by seeming.

He deemed it unmeet to draw back & hide him, so he went forth past them toward the house. The King's Son scowled on him as he passed, but the Lady, over whose beauteous face flickered the joyous morning smiles, took no more heed of him than if he had been one of the trees of the wood. But she had been so high and disdainful with him the evening before, that he thought little of that. The twain went on, skirting the hazel-copse, and he could not choose but turn his eyes on them, so sorely did the Lady's beauty draw them. Then befell another thing; for behind them the boughs of the hazels parted, and there stood that little evil thing, he or another of his kind; for he was quite unclad, save by his fell of yellowy-brown hair, and that he was girt with a leathern girdle, wherein was stuck an ugly two-edged knife: he stood upright a moment, and cast his eyes at Walter & grinned, but not as if he knew him; and scarce could Walter say whether it were the one he had seen, or another: then he cast himself down on his belly, and fell to creeping through the long grass like a serpent, following the footsteps of the Lady and her lover; and now, as he crept, Walter deemed, in his loathing, that the creature was liker to a ferret than aught else. He crept on marvellous swiftly, and was soon clean out of sight. But Walter stood staring after him for a while, and then lay down by the copse-side, that he might watch the house and the entry thereof; for he thought, now perchance presently will the kind maiden come hither to comfort me with a word or two. But hour passed by hour, and still she came not;

and still he lay there, and thought of the Maid, and longed for her kindness & wisdom, till he could not refrain his tears, & wept for the lack of her. Then he arose, and went and sat in the porch, and was very downcast of mood.

BUT as he sat there, back comes the Lady again, the King's Son leading her by the hand; they entered the porch, and she passed by him so close that the odour of her raiment filled all the air about him, and the sleekness of her side nigh touched him, so that he could not fail to note that her garments were somewhat disarrayed, & that she kept her right hand (for her left the King's Son held) to her bosom to hold the cloth together there, whereas the rich raiment had been torn off from her right shoulder. As they passed by him, the King's Son once more scowled on him, wordless, but even more fiercely than before; and again the Lady heeded him nought.

AFTER they had gone on a while, he entered the hall, and found it empty from end to end, and no sound in it save the tinkling of the fountain; but there was victual set on the board. He ate & drank thereof to keep life lusty within him, & then went out again to the wood-side to watch and to long; and the time hung heavy on his hands because of the lack of the fair Maiden.

HE was of mind not to go into the house to his rest that night, but to sleep under the boughs of the forest. But a little after sunset he saw a bright-clad image moving amidst the carven images of the porch, and the King's Son came forth & went straight to him, and said: Thou art to enter the house, and go into thy chamber forthwith, and by no means to go forth of it betwixt sunset and sunrise. My Lady will not away with thy prowling round the house in the night-tide.

Therewith he turned away, & went into the house again; and Walter followed him soberly, remembering how the Maid had bidden him forbear. So he went to his chamber, and slept.

BUT amidst of the night he awoke and deemed that he heard a voice not far off, so he crept out of his bed & peered around, lest, perchance, the Maid had come to speak with him; but his chamber was dusk and empty: then he went to the window and looked out, and saw the moon shining bright and white upon the greensward. And lo! the Lady walking with the King's Son, & he clad in thin and wanton raiment, but she in nought else save what God had given her of long, crispy yellow hair. Then was Walter ashamed to look on her, seeing that there was a man with her, and gat him back to his bed; but yet a long while ere he slept again he had the image before his eyes of the fair woman on the dewy moonlit grass.

THE next day matters went much the same way, and the next also, save that his sorrow was increased, and he sickened sorely of hope deferred. On the fourth day also the forenoon wore as erst; but in the heat of the afternoon Walter sought to the hazel-copse, and laid him down there hard by a little clearing thereof, and slept from very weariness of grief. There, after a while, he woke with words still hanging in his ears, & he knew at once that it was they twain talking together.

The King's Son had just done his say, and now it

was the Lady beginning in her honey-sweet voice, low but strong, wherein even was a little of huskiness; she said: Otto, belike it were well to have a little patience, till we find out what the man is, & whence he cometh; it will always be easy to rid us of him; it is but a word to our Dwarf-king, & it will be done in a few minutes.

Patience! said the King's Son, angrily; I wot not how to have patience with him; for I can see of him that he is rude and violent and headstrong, & a low-born wily one. Forsooth, he had patience enough with me the other even, when I rated him in, like the dog that he is, & he had no manhood to say one word to me. Soothly, as he followed after me, I had a mind to turn about & deal him a buffet on the face, to see if I could but draw one angry word from him.

The Lady laughed, and said: Well, Otto, I know not; that which thou deemest dastardy in him may be but prudence and wisdom, and he an alien, far from his friends and nigh to his foes. Perchance we shall yet try him what he is. Meanwhile, I rede thee try him not with buffets, save he be weaponless & with bounden hands; or else I deem that but a little while shalt thou be fain of thy blow.

NOW when Walter heard her words and the voice wherein they were said, he might not forbear being stirred by them, and to him, all lonely there, they seemed friendly.

But he lay still, and the King's Son answered the Lady and said: I know not what is in thine heart concerning this runagate, that thou shouldst bemock me with his valiancy, whereof thou knowest nought. If thou deem me unworthy of thee, send me back

57

safe to my father's country; I may look to have worship there; yea, and the love of fair women belike.

Therewith it seemed as if he had put forth his hand to the Lady to caress her, for she said: Nay, lay not thine hand on my shoulder, for today and now it is not the hand of love, but of pride & folly, and would-be mastery. Nay, neither shalt thou rise up & leave me until thy mood is softer and kinder to me.

THEN was there silence betwixt them a while, and thereafter the King's Son spake in a wheedling voice: My goddess, I pray thee pardon me! But canst thou wonder that I fear thy wearying of me, and am therefore peevish and jealous? thou so far above the Queens of the World, and I a poor youth that without thee were nothing!

She answered nought, and he went on again: Was it not so, O goddess, that this man of the sons of the merchants was little heedful of thee, and thy loveliness & thy majesty?

She laughed & said: Maybe he deemed not that he had much to gain of us, seeing thee sitting by our side, and whereas we spake to him coldly and sternly & disdainfully. Withal, the poor youth was dazzled and shamefaced before us; that we could see in the eyes and the mien of him.

NOW this she spoke so kindly & sweetly, that again was Walter all stirred thereat; and it came into his mind that it might be she knew he was anigh and hearing her, and that she spake as much for him as for the King's Son: but that one answered: Lady, didst thou not see somewhat else in his eyes, to wit, that they had but of late looked on some fair woman other than thee? As for me, I deem it not so unlike that on the way to thine hall he may have fallen in with thy Maid.

He spoke in a faltering voice, as if shrinking from some storm that might come. And forsooth the Lady's voice was changed as she answered, though there was no outward heat in it; rather it was sharp and eager and cold at once. She said: Yea, that is not ill thought of; but we may not always keep our thrall in mind. If it be so as thou deemest, we shall come to know it most like when we next fall in with her; or if she hath been shy this time, then shall she pay the heavier for it; for we will question her by the fountain in the Hall as to what betid by the Fountain of the Rock.

Spake the King's Son, faltering yet more: Lady, were it not better to question the man himself? the Maid is stout-hearted, & will not be speedily quelled into a true tale; whereas the man I deem of no account.

No, no, said the Lady sharply, it shall not be.

Then was she silent a while; & then she said: How if the man should prove to be our master?

Nay, our Lady, said the King's Son, thou art jesting with me; thou and thy might and thy wisdom, and all that thy wisdom may command, to be over-mastered by a gangrel churl!

But how if I will not have it command, King's Son? said the Lady: I tell thee I know thine heart, but thou knowest not mine. But be at peace! For since thou hast prayed for this woman . . . nay, not with thy words, I wot, but with thy trembling hands, & thine anxious eyes, and knitted brow . . . I say, since thou hast prayed for her so earnestly, she shall escape this time. But whether it will be to her gain in the long run, I misdoubt me. See thou to that, Otto!

thou who hast held me in thine arms so oft. And now thou mayest depart if thou wilt.

T seemed to Walter as if the King's Son were dumbfoundered at her words: he answered nought, and presently he rose from the ground, and went his ways slowly toward the house. The Lady lay there a little while, & then went her ways also; but turned away from the house toward the wood at the other end thereof, whereby Walter had first come thither.

S for Walter, he was confused in mind and shaken in spirit; and withal he seemed to see guile & cruel deeds under the talk of those two, and waxed wrathful thereat. Yet he said to himself, that nought might he do, but was as one bound hand and foot, till he had seen the Maid again.

CHAPTER XIII ⁄ NOW IS THE HUNT UP

EXT morning was he up betimes, but he was cast down and heavy of heart, not looking for aught else to betide than had betid those last four days. But otherwise it fell out; for when he came down into the hall, there was the Lady sitting on the high-seat all alone, clad but in a coat of white linen; & she turned her head when she heard his footsteps, & looked on him, & greeted him, and said: Come hither, guest.

So he went and stood before her, and she said: Though as yet thou hast had no welcome here, & no honour, it hath not entered into thine heart to flee

60

from us; and to say sooth, that is well for thee, for flee away from our hand thou mightest not, nor mightest thou depart without our furtherance. But for this we can thee thank, that thou hast abided here our bidding, & eaten thine heart through the heavy wearing of four days, and made no plaint. Yet I cannot deem thee a dastard; thou so well knit and shapely of body, so clear-eyed and bold of visage. Wherefore now I ask thee, art thou willing to do me service, thereby to earn thy guesting?

WALTER answered her, somewhat faltering at first, for he was astonished at the change which had come over her; for now she spoke to him in friendly wise, though indeed as a great lady would speak to a young man ready to serve her in all honour. Said he: Lady, I can thee thank humbly and heartily in that thou biddest me do thee service; for these days past I have loathed the emptiness of the hours, and nought better could I ask for than to serve so glorious a Mistress in all honour.

She frowned somewhat, and said: Thou shalt not call me Mistress; there is but one who so calleth me, that is my thrall; & thou art none such. Thou shalt call me Lady, and I shall be well pleased that thou be my squire, and for this present thou shalt serve me in the hunting. So get thy gear; take thy bow and arrows, and gird thee to thy sword. For in this fair land may one find beasts more perilous than be buck or hart. I go now to array me; we will depart while the day is yet young; for so make we the summer day the fairest.

E made obeisance to her, and she arose & went to her chamber, and Walter dight himself, and then abode her in the porch; and in less than an hour she came out of the hall, and Walter's heart beat when he saw that the Maid followed her hard at heel, and scarce might he school his eyes not to gaze over-eagerly at his dear friend. She was clad even as she was before, and was changed in no wise, save that love troubled her face when she first beheld him, & she had much ado to master it: howbeit the Mistress heeded not the trouble of her, or made no semblance of heeding it, till the Maiden's face was all according to its wont.

UT this Walter found strange, that after all that disdain of the Maid's thralldom which he had heard of the Mistress, and after all the threats against her, now was the Mistress become mild and debonaire to her, as a good lady to her good maiden. When Walter bowed the knee to her, she turned unto the Maid, and said: Look thou, my Maid, at this fair new Squire that I have gotten! Will not he be valiant in the greenwood? And see whether he be well shapen or not. Doth he not touch thine heart, when thou thinkest of all the woe, and fear, and trouble of the World beyond the Wood, which he hath escaped, to dwell in this little land peaceably, and well-beloved both by the Mistress & the Maid? And thou, my Squire, look a little at this fair slim Maiden, and say if she pleaseth thee not: didst thou deem that we had any thing so fair in this lonely place?

RANK and kind was the smile on her radiant visage, nor did she seem to note any whit the trouble on Walter's face, nor how he strove to keep his eyes from the Maid. As for her, she had so wholly mastered her countenance, that belike she used her face guilefully, for she stood as one humble but happy, with a smile on her face, blushing, and with her head hung down as if shamefaced before a goodly young man, a stranger.

But the Lady looked upon her kindly & said: Come hither, child, and fear not this frank and free young man, who belike feareth thee a little, & full certainly feareth me; and yet only after the manner of men.

And therewith she took the Maid by the hand and drew her to her, & pressed her to her bosom, & kissed her cheeks and her lips, and undid the lacing of her gown & bared a shoulder of her, and swept away her skirt from her feet; and then turned to Walter and said: Lo thou, Squire! is not this a lovely thing to have grown up amongst our rough oak-boles? What! art thou looking at the iron ring there? It is nought, save a token that she is mine, and that I may not be without her.

Then she took the Maid by the shoulders and turned her about as in sport, and said: Go thou now, & bring hither the good grey ones; for needs must we bring home some venison today, whereas this stout warrior may not feed on nought save manchets and honey.

O the Maid went her way, taking care, as Walter deemed, to give no side glance to him. But he stood there shamefaced, so confused with all this open-hearted kindness of the great Lady & with the fresh sight of the darling beauty of the Maid, that he went nigh to thinking that all he had heard since he had come to the porch of the house that first time was but a dream of evil.

BUT while he stood pondering these matters, and staring before him as one mazed, the Lady laughed out in his face, and touched him on the arm & said: Ah, our Squire, is it so that now thou hast seen my Maid thou wouldst with a good will abide behind to talk with her? But call to mind thy word pledged to me e'en now! And more-over I tell thee this for thy behoof now she is out of ear-shot, that I will above all things take thee away to-day: for there be other eyes, & they nought un-comely, that look at whiles on my fair-ankled thrall; & who knows but the swords might be out if I take not the better heed, and give thee not every whit of thy will.

AS she spoke and moved forward, he turned a little, so that now the edge of that hazel coppice was within his eye-shot, & he deemed that once more he saw the yellow-brown evil thing crawling forth from the thicket; then, turning suddenly on the Lady, he met her eyes, and seemed in one moment of time to find a far other look in them than that of frankness and kindness; though in a flash they changed back again, and she said merrily and sweetly: So so, Sir Squire, now art thou awake again, & mayest for a little while look on me.

NOW it came into his head, with that look of hers, all that might befall him and the Maid if he mastered not his passion, nor did what he might to dissemble; so he bent the knee to her, and spoke boldly to her in her own vein, and said: Nay, most gracious of ladies, never would I abide behind to-day since thou farest afield. But if my speech be hampered, or mine eyes stray, is it not because my mind is confused by thy beauty, & the honey of kind words which floweth from thy mouth?

She laughed outright at his word, but not disdain-fully, and said: This is well spoken, Squire, and even what a squire should say to his liege lady, when the sun is up on a fair morning, and she and he and all the world are glad.

She stood quite near him as she spoke, her hand was on his shoulder, and her eyes shone and sparkled. Sooth to say, that excusing of his confusion was like enough in seeming to the truth; for sure never creature was fashioned fairer than she: clad she was for the greenwood as the hunting-goddess of the Gentiles, with her green gown gathered unto her girdle, & sandals on her feet; a bow in her hand and a quiver at her back: she was taller and bigger of fashion than the dear Maiden, whiter of flesh, and more glorious, and brighter of hair; as a flower of flowers for fairness and fragrance.

SHE said: Thou art verily a fair squire before the hunt is up, & if thou be as good in the hunting, all will be better than well, and the guest will be welcome. But lo! here cometh our Maid with the good grey ones. Go meet her, and we will tarry no longer than for thy taking the leash in hand.

So Walter looked, and saw the Maid coming with two couple of great hounds in the leash straining against her as she came along. He ran lightly to meet her, wondering if he should have a look, or a half-whisper from her; but she let him take the white thongs from her hand, with the same half-smile of shamefacedness still set on her face, &, going past him, came softly up to the Lady, swaying like a willow-branch in the wind, and stood before her, with her arms hanging down by her sides. Then the Lady turned to her, and said: Look to thyself, our Maid, while we are away. This fair young man thou needest not to fear indeed, for he is good and leal; but what thou shalt do with the King's Son I wot not. He is a hot lover forsooth, but a hard man; and whiles evil is his mood, & perilous both to thee and me. And if thou do his will, it shall be ill for thee; & if thou do it not, take heed of him, and let me, and me only, come between his wrath and thee. I may do somewhat for thee. Even yesterday he was instant with me to have thee chastised after the manner of thralls; but I bade him keep silence of such words, and jeered him & mocked him, till he went away from me peevish & in anger. So look to it that thou fall not into any trap of his contrivance.

THEN the Maid cast herself at the Mistress's feet, & kissed & embraced them; and as she rose up, the Lady laid her hand lightly on her head, and then, turning to Walter, cried out: Now Squire, let us leave all these troubles and wiles and desires behind us, and flit through the merry green-wood like the Gentiles of old days.

And therewith she drew up the laps of her gown till the whiteness of her knees was seen, and set off swiftly toward the wood that lay south of the house, and Walter followed, marvelling at her goodliness; nor durst he cast a look backward to the Maiden, for he knew that she desired him, & it was her only that he looked to for his deliverance from this house of guile and lies.

CHAPTER XIV ⁄ THE HUNTING OF THE HART

S they went, they found a change in the land, which grew emptier of big and wide⁄spreading trees, & more beset with thickets. From one of these they roused a hart, and Walter let slip his hounds thereafter, & he and the Lady followed running. Exceeding swift was she, & well⁄breathed withal, so that Walter wondered at her; and eager she was in the chase as the very hounds, heeding nothing the scratching of briars or the whipping of stiff twigs as she sped on. But for all their eager hunting, the quarry outran both dogs and folk, and gat him into a great thicket, amidmost whereof was a wide plash of water. Into the thicket they followed him, but he took to the water under their eyes and made land on the other side; and because of the tangle of underwood, he swam across much faster than they might have any hope to come round on him; and so were the hunters left undone for that time.

O the Lady cast herself down on the green grass anigh the water, while Walter blew the hounds in and coupled them up; then he turned round to her, & lo! she was weeping for despite that they had lost the quarry; and again did Walter wonder that so little a matter should raise a passion of tears in her. He durst not ask what ailed her, or proffer her solace, but was not ill apaid by beholding her loveliness as there she lay.

P RESENTLY she raised up her head and turned to Walter, and spake to him angrily and said: Squire, why dost thou stand staring at me like a fool?

Yea, Lady, he said; but the sight of thee maketh me foolish to do aught else but to look on thee.

She said, in a peevish voice: Tush, Squire, the day is too far spent for soft and courtly speeches; what was good there is nought so good here. Withal, I know more of thine heart than thou deemest.

Walter hung down his head and reddened, and she looked on him, and her face changed, and she smiled & said, kindly this time: Look ye, Squire, I am hot and weary, and ill-content; but presently it will be better with me; for my knees have been telling my shoulders that the cold water of this little lake will be sweet & pleasant this summer noonday, and that I shall forget my foil when I have taken my pleasure therein. Wherefore, go thou with thine hounds without the thicket and there abide my coming. And I bid thee look not aback as thou goest, for therein were peril to thee: I shall not keep thee tarrying long alone.

H E bowed his head to her, and turned and went his ways. And now, when he was a little space away from her, he deemed her indeed a marvel of women, and well-nigh forgat all his doubts & fears concerning her, whether she were a fair image fashioned out of lies and guile, or it might

68

be but an evil thing in the shape of a goodly woman. Forsooth, when he saw her caressing the dear and friendly Maid, his heart all turned against her, despite what his eyes & his ears told his mind, & she seemed like as it were a serpent enfolding the simplicity of the body which he loved.

But now it was all changed, and he lay on the grass and longed for her coming; which was delayed for somewhat more than an hour. Then she came back to him, smiling & fresh and cheerful, her green gown let down to her heels.

He sprang up to meet her, & she came close to him, and spake from a laughing face: Squire, hast thou no meat in thy wallet? For, meseemeth, I fed thee when thou wert hungry the other day; do thou now the same by me.

He smiled, and louted to her, and took his wallet and brought out thence bread and flesh and wine, & spread them all out before her on the green grass, and then stood by humbly before her. But she said: Nay, my Squire, sit down by me & eat with me, for to-day are we both hunters together.

So he sat down by her trembling, but neither for awe of her greatness, nor for fear & horror of her guile and sorcery.

A WHILE they sat there together after they had done their meat, & the Lady fell a-talking with Walter concerning the parts of the earth, and the manners of men, & of his journeyings to and fro.

At last she said: Thou hast told me much and answered all my questions wisely, and as my good Squire should, and that pleaseth me. But now tell me of the city wherein thou wert born & bred; a city whereof thou hast hitherto told me nought.

Lady, he said, it is a fair and a great city, & to many it seemeth lovely. But I have left it, and now it is nothing to me.

Hast thou not kindred there? said she.

Yea, said he, and foemen withal; and a false woman waylayeth my life there.

And what was she? said the Lady.

Said Walter: She was but my wife.

Was she fair? said the Lady.

Walter looked on her a while, and then said: I was going to say that she was well-nigh as fair as thou; but that may scarce be. Yet was she very fair. But now, kind and gracious Lady, I will say this word to thee: I marvel that thou askest so many things concerning the city of Langton on Holm, where I was born, and where are my kindred yet; for meseemeth that thou knowest it thyself.

I know it, I? said the Lady.

What, then! thou knowest it not? said Walter.

Spake the Lady, and some of her old disdain was in her words: Dost thou deem that I wander about the world & its cheaping-steads like one of the chapmen? Nay, I dwell in the Wood beyond the World, & nowhere else. What hath put this word into thy mouth?

He said: Pardon me, Lady, if I have misdone; but thus it was: Mine own eyes beheld thee going down the quays of our city, and thence a ship-board, & the ship sailed out of the haven. And first of all went a strange dwarf, whom I have seen here, and then thy Maid; and then went thy gracious and lovely body.

THE Lady's face changed as he spoke, and she turned red and then pale, & set her teeth; but she refrained her, & said: Squire, I see of thee that thou art no liar, nor light of wit, therefore I suppose that thou hast verily seen some appearance of me; but never have I been in Langton, nor thought thereof, nor known that such a stead there was until thou namedst it e'en now. Wherefore, I deem that an enemy hath cast the shadow of me on the air of that land.

Yea, my Lady, said Walter; and what enemy mightest thou have to have done this?

She was slow of answer, but spake at last from a quivering mouth of anger: Knowest thou not the saw, that a man's foes are they of his own house? If I find out for a truth who hath done this, the said enemy shall have an evil hour with me.

AGAIN she was silent, and she clenched her hand & strained her limbs in the heat of her anger; so that Walter was afraid of her, and all his misgivings came back to his heart again, & he repented that he had told her so much. But in a little while all that trouble and wrath seemed to flow off her, and again was she of good cheer, and kind and sweet to him; and she said: But in sooth, however it may be, I thank thee, my Squire and friend, for telling me hereof. And surely no wyte do I lay on thee. And, moreover, is it not this vision which hath brought thee hither?

So it is, Lady, said he.

Then have we to thank it, said the Lady, & thou art welcome to our land.

And therewith she held out her hand to him, and

he took it on his knees and kissed it; & then it was as if a red-hot iron had run through his heart, and he felt faint, & bowed down his head. But he held her hand yet, & kissed it many times, and the wrist and the arm, and knew not where he was.

BUT she drew a little away from him, and arose and said: Now is the day wearing, and if we are to bear back any venison we must buckle to the work. So arise, Squire, and take the hounds and come with me; for not far off is a little thicket which mostly harbours foison of deer, great & small. Let us come our ways.

CHAPTER XV ⁄ THE SLAYING OF THE QUARRY

SO they walked on quietly thence some half a mile, and ever the Lady would have Walter to walk by her side, & not follow a little behind her, as was meet for a servant to do; & she touched his hand at whiles as she showed him beast and fowl and tree, and the sweetness of her body overcame him, so that for a while he thought of nothing save her.

NOW when they were come to the thicket-side, she turned to him & said: Squire, I am no ill wood-man, so that thou mayst trust me that we shall not be brought to shame the second time; and I shall do sagely: so nock an arrow to thy bow, and abide me here, & stir not hence; for I shall enter this thicket without the hounds, and arouse the quarry for thee; and see that thou be brisk and clean⁄shooting, and then shalt thou have a reward of me.

Therewith she drew up her skirts through her girdle again, took her bent bow in her hand, and drew an arrow out of the quiver, and stepped lightly into the thicket, leaving him longing for the sight of her, as he hearkened to the tread of her feet on the dry leaves, and the rustling of the brake as she thrust through it.

Thus he stood for a few minutes, and then he heard a kind of gibbering cry without words, yet as of a woman, coming from the thicket, & while his heart was yet gathering the thought that something had gone amiss, he glided swiftly, but with little stir, into the brake.

HE had gone but a little way ere he saw the Lady standing there in a narrow clearing, her face pale as death, her knees cleaving to⁄gether, her body swaying and tottering, her hands hanging down, and the bow and arrow fallen to the ground; and ten yards before her a great⁄headed yellow creature crouching flat to the earth and slowly drawing nigher.

He stopped short; one arrow was already notched to the string, & another hung loose to the lesser fingers of his string⁄hand. He raised his right hand, & drew & loosed in a twinkling; the shaft flew close to the Lady's side, and straight way all the wood rung with a huge roar, as the yellow lion turned about to bite at the shaft which had sunk deep into him behind the shoulder, as if a bolt out of the heavens had smitten him. But straightway had Walter loosed again, & then, throwing down his bow, he ran forward with his drawn sword gleaming in his hand, while the lion weltered and rolled, but had no might to move forward. Then Walter went up to him warily & thrust him through to the heart, & leapt aback, lest the beast might yet have life in him to smite; but he left his struggling, his huge voice died out, and he lay there moveless before the hunter.

WALTER abode a little, facing him, & then turned about to the Lady, and she had fallen down in a heap whereas she stood, and lay there all huddled up and voiceless. So he knelt down by her, and lifted up her head, and bade her arise, for the foe was slain. And after a little she stretched out her limbs, & turned about on the grass, & seemed to sleep, and the colour came into her face again, & it grew soft and a little smiling. Thus she lay awhile, and Walter sat by her watching her, till at last she opened her eyes and sat up, and knew him, and smiling on him said: What hath befallen, Squire, that I have slept & dreamed?

He answered nothing, till her memory came back to her, and then she arose, trembling and pale, & said: Let us leave this wood, for the Enemy is therein.

And she hastened away before him till they came out at the thicket-side whereas the hounds had been left, & they were standing there uneasy and whining; so Walter coupled them, while the Lady stayed not, but went away swiftly homeward, and Walter followed.

AT last she stayed her swift feet, and turned round on Walter, and said: Squire, come hither!

So did he, and she said: I am weary again; let us sit under this quicken-tree, and rest us.

So they sat down, and she sat looking between her knees a while; and at last she said: Why didst thou not bring the lion's hide?

He said: Lady, I will go back and flay the beast, and bring on the hide.

And he arose therewith, but she caught him by the skirts and drew him down, and said: Nay, thou shalt not go; abide with me. Sit down again.

He did so, and she said: Thou shalt not go from me; for I am afraid: I am not used to looking on the face of death.

She grew pale as she spoke, & set a hand to her breast, & sat so a while without speaking. At last she turned to him smiling, & said: How was it with the aspect of me when I stood before the peril of the Enemy?

And she laid a hand upon his.

O gracious one, quoth he, thou wert, as ever, full lovely, but I feared for thee.

She moved not her hand from his, and she said: Good and true Squire, I said ere I entered the thicket e'en now that I would reward thee if thou slewest the quarry. He is dead, though thou hast left the skin behind upon the carcase. Ask now thy reward, but take time to think what it shall be.

He felt her hand warm upon his, and drew in the sweet odour of her mingled with the woodland scents under the hot sun of the afternoon, & his heart was clouded with manlike desire of her. And it was a near thing but he had spoken, and craved of her the reward of the freedom of her Maid, and that he might depart with her into other lands; but as his mind wavered betwixt this & that, the Lady, who had been eyeing

75

him keenly, drew her hand away from him; & therewith doubt & fear flowed into his mind, & he refrained
him of speech.

Then she laughed merrily & said: The good Squire
is shamefaced; he feareth a lady more than a lion.
Will it be a reward to thee if I bid thee to kiss my
cheek?

Therewith she leaned her face toward him, and he
kissed her well-favouredly, and then sat gazing on her,
wondering what should betide to him on the morrow.

 HEN she arose & said: Come Squire, and
let us home; be not abashed, there shall be
other rewards hereafter.

So they went their ways quietly; and it was nigh
sunset against they entered the house again. Walter
looked round for the Maid, but beheld her not; & the
Lady said to him: I go to my chamber, & now is thy
service over for this day.

Then she nodded to him friendly and went her
ways.

CHAPTER XVI · OF THE KING'S SON & THE MAID

UT as for Walter, he went out of
the house again, and fared slowly
over the woodlawns till he came to
another close thicket or brake; he
entered from mere wantonness, or
that he might be the more apart &
hidden, so as to think over his case. There he lay
down under the thick boughs, but could not so herd

his thoughts that they would dwell steady in looking into what might come to him within the next days; rather visions of those two women & the monster did but float before him, and fear and desire & the hope of life ran to and fro in his mind.

AS he lay thus he heard footsteps drawing near, and he looked between the boughs, and though the sun had just set, he could see close by him a man & a woman going slowly, & they hand in hand; at first he deemed it would be the King's Son & the Lady, but presently he saw that it was the King's Son indeed, but that it was the Maid whom he was holding by the hand. And now he saw of him that his eyes were bright with desire, and of her that she was very pale. Yet when he heard her begin to speak, it was in a steady voice that she said: King's Son, thou hast threatened me oft and unkindly, and now thou threatenest me again, and no less unkindly. But whatever were thy need herein before, now is there no more need; for my Mistress, of whom thou wert weary, is now grown weary of thee, & belike will not now reward me for drawing thy love to me, as once she would have done; to wit, before the coming of this stranger. Therefore I say, since I am but a thrall, poor and helpless, betwixt you two mighty ones, I have no choice but to do thy will.

As she spoke she looked all round about her, as one distraught by the anguish of fear. Walter, amidst of his wrath and grief, had well-nigh drawn his sword & rushed out of his lair upon the King's Son. But he deemed it sure that, so doing, he should undo the Maid altogether, and himself also belike, so he refrained him, though it were a hard matter.

HE Maid had stayed her feet now close to where Walter lay, some five yards from him only, and he doubted whether she saw him not from where she stood. As to the King's Son, he was so intent upon the Maid, and so greedy of her beauty, that it was not like that he saw anything.

Now moreover Walter looked, & deemed that he beheld something through the grass and bracken on the other side of those two, an ugly brown and yellow body, which, if it were not some beast of the foumart kind, must needs be the monstrous dwarf, or one of his kin; and the flesh crept upon Walter's bones with the horror of him.

But the King's Son spoke unto the Maid: Sweetling, I shall take the gift thou givest me, neither shall I threaten thee any more, howbeit thou givest it not very gladly or graciously.

She smiled on him with her lips alone, for her eyes were wandering and haggard. My lord, she said, is not this the manner of women?

Well, he said, I say that I will take thy love even so given. Yet let me hear again that thou lovest not that vile newcomer, & that thou hast not seen him, save this morning along with my Lady. Nay now, thou shalt swear it.

What shall I swear by? she said.

Quoth he, thou shalt swear by my body; & therewith he thrust himself close up against her; but she drew her hand from his, & laid it on his breast, and said: I swear it by thy body.

He smiled on her licorously, and took her by the shoulders, and kissed her face many times, & then stood aloof from her, and said: Now have I had hansel:

but tell me, when shall I come to thee?

She spoke out clearly: Within three days at furthest; I will do thee to wit of the day and the hour to-morrow, or the day after.

He kissed her once more, and said: Forget it not, or the threat holds good.

And therewith he turned about and went his ways toward the house; & Walter saw the yellow-brown thing creeping after him in the gathering dusk.

AS for the Maid, she stood for a while without moving, and looking after the King's Son & the creature that followed him. Then she turned about to where Walter lay and lightly put aside the boughs, and Walter leapt up, and they stood face to face. She said softly but eagerly: Friend, touch me not yet!

He spake not, but looked on her sternly. She said: Thou art angry with me?

Still he spake not; but she said: Friend, this at least I will pray thee; not to play with life & death; with happiness and misery. Dost thou not remember the oath which we swore each to each but a little while ago? And dost thou deem that I have changed in these few days? Is thy mind concerning thee and me the same as it was? If it be not so, now tell me. For now have I the mind to do as if neither thou nor I are changed to each other, whoever may have kissed mine unwilling lips, or whomsoever thy lips may have kissed. But if thou hast changed, and wilt no longer give me thy love, nor crave mine, then shall this steel (& she drew a sharp knife from her girdle) be for the fool and the dastard who hath made thee wroth with me, my friend, & my friend that I deemed I had won.

And then let come what will come! But if thou be nought changed, & the oath yet holds, then, when a little while hath passed, may we thrust all evil and guile and grief behind us, and long joy shall lie before us, and long life, & all honour in death: if only thou wilt do as I bid thee, O my dear, and my friend, and my first friend!

HE looked on her, and his breast heaved up as all the sweetness of her kind love took hold on him, and his face changed, & the tears filled his eyes and ran over, and rained down before her, and he stretched out his hand toward her.

Then she said exceeding sweetly: Now indeed I see that it is well with me, yea, & with thee also. A sore pain it is to me, that not even now may I take thine hand, and cast mine arms about thee, and kiss the lips that love me. But so it has to be. My dear, even so I were fain to stand here long before thee, even if we spake no more word to each other; but abiding here is perilous; for there is ever an evil spy upon my doings, who has now as I deem followed the King's Son to the house, but who will return when he has tracked him home thither: so we must sunder. But belike there is yet time for a word or two: first, the rede which I had thought on for our deliverance is now afoot, though I durst not tell thee thereof, nor have time thereto. But this much shall I tell thee, that whereas great is the craft of my Mistress in wizardry, yet I also have some little craft therein, and this, which she hath not, to change the aspect of folk so utterly that they seem other than they verily are; yea, so that one may have the aspect of another. Now the next thing is this: whatso-ever my Mistress may bid thee, do her will therein with no more nay-saying than thou deemest may please her. And the next thing: wheresoever thou mayst meet me, speak not to me, make no sign to me, even when I seem to be all alone, till I stoop down and touch the ring on my ankle with my right hand; but if I do so, then stay thee, without fail, till I speak. The last thing I will say to thee, dear friend, ere we both go our ways, this it is. When we are free, and thou knowest all that I have done, I pray thee deem me not evil & wicked, and be not wroth with me for my deed; whereas thou wottest well that I am not in like plight with other women. I have heard tell that when the knight goeth to the war, and hath overcome his foes by the shearing of swords and guileful tricks, & hath come back home to his own folk, they praise him & bless him, and crown him with flowers, and boast of him before God in the minster for his deliverance of friend and folk and city. Why shouldst thou be worse to me than this? Now is all said, my dear and my friend; farewell, farewell!

HEREWITH she turned & went her ways toward the house in all speed, but making somewhat of a compass. And when she was gone, Walter knelt down and kissed the place where her feet had been, & arose thereafter, & made his way toward the house, he also, but slowly, and staying oft on his way.

CHAPTER XVII ⁄ OF THE HOUSE AND THE PLEASANCE IN THE WOOD

N the morrow morning Walter loitered a while about the house till the morn was grown old, and then about noon he took his bow and arrows and went into the woods to the northward, to get him some venison. He went somewhat far ere he shot him a fawn, & then he sat him down to rest under the shade of a great chestnut tree, for it was not far past the hottest of the day. He looked around thence and saw below him a little dale with a pleasant stream running through it, and he bethought him of bathing therein, so he went down & had his pleasure of the water and the willowy banks; for he lay naked a while on the grass by the lip of the water, for joy of the flickering shade, and the little breeze that ran over the down⁄long ripples of the stream.

Then he did on his raiment, and began to come his ways up the bent, but had scarce gone three steps ere he saw a woman coming towards him from down⁄stream. His heart came into his mouth when he saw her, for she stooped & reached down on her ankle, so that at first he deemed it had been the Maid, but at the second eyeshot he saw that it was the Mistress. She stood still and looked on him, so that he deemed she would have him come to her. So he went to meet her, and grew somewhat shamefaced as he drew nigher, & wondered at her, for now was she clad but in one garment of some dark grey silky stuff, embroidered with, as it were, a garland of flowers about the middle, but which was so thin that, as the wind drifted it from side and limb, it hid her no more, but for the said garland, than if water were running over her: her face was full of smiling joy & content as she spake to him in a kind, caressing voice, and said: I give thee good day, good Squire, & well art thou met. And she held out her hand to him. He knelt down before her and kissed it, and abode still upon his knees, & hanging down his head.

But she laughed outright, and stooped down to him, & put her hand to his arms, & raised him up, and said to him: What is this, my Squire, that thou kneelest to me as to an idol?

He said faltering: I wot not; but perchance thou art an idol; and I fear thee.

What! she said, more than yesterday, whenas thou sawest me afraid?

Said he: Yea, for that now I see thee unhidden, & meseemeth there hath been none such since the old days of the Gentiles.

She said: Hast thou not yet bethought thee of a gift to crave of me, a reward for the slaying of mine enemy, and the saving of me from death?

O my Lady, he said, even so much would I have done for any other lady, or, forsooth, for any poor man; for so my manhood would have bidden me. Speak not of gifts to me then. Moreover (and he reddened therewith, & his voice faltered), didst thou not give me my sweet reward yesterday? What more durst I ask?

HE held her peace awhile, & looked on him keenly; & he reddened under her gaze. Then wrath came into her face, and she reddened &

knit her brows, and spake to him in a voice of anger, & said: Nay, what is this? It is growing in my mind that thou deemest the gift of me unworthy! Thou, an alien, an outcast; one endowed with the little wisdom of the World without the Wood! And here I stand before thee, all glorious in my nakedness, & so fulfilled of wisdom, that I can make this wilderness to any whom I love more full of joy than the kingdoms & cities of the world . . . and thou! . . . Ah, but it is the Enemy that hath done this, & made the guileless guileful! Yet will I have the upper hand at least, though thou suffer for it, and I suffer for thee.

ALTER stood before her with hanging head, & he put forth his hands as if praying off her anger, and pondered what answer he should make; for now he feared for himself and the Maid; so at last he looked up to her, and said boldly: Nay, Lady, I know what thy words mean, whereas I remember thy first welcome of me. I wot, forsooth, that thou wouldst call me base-born, and of no account, and unworthy to touch the hem of thy raiment; and that I have been over-bold, and guilty towards thee; & doubtless this is sooth, and I have deserved thine anger: but I will not ask thee to pardon me, for I have done but what I must needs. She looked on him calmly now, and without any wrath, but rather as if she would read what was written in his inmost heart. Then her face changed into joyousness again, and she smote her palms together, & cried out: This is but foolish talk; for yesterday did I see thy valiancy, and to-day I have seen thy goodliness; and I say, that though thou mightest not be good enough for a fool woman of the earthly baronage, yet art thou good enough for me, the wise and the mighty, & the lovely. And whereas thou sayest that I gave thee but disdain when first thou camest to us, grudge not against me therefor, because it was done but to prove thee; and now thou art proven.

HEN again he knelt down before her, and embraced her knees, and again she raised him up, and let her arm hang down over his shoulder, and her cheek brush his cheek; and she kissed his mouth and said: Hereby is all forgiven, both thine offence & mine; and now cometh joy and merry days.

HEREWITH her smiling face grew grave, & she stood before him looking stately & gracious and kind at once, and she took his hand & said: Thou mightest deem my chamber in the Golden House of the Wood over queenly, since thou art no masterful man. So now hast thou chosen well the place wherein to meet me to-day, for hard by on the other side of the stream is a bower of pleasance, which, forsooth, not every one who cometh to this land may find; there shall I be to thee as one of the up-country damsels of thine own land, and thou shalt not be abashed.

She sidled up to him as she spoke, and would he, would he not, her sweet voice tickled his very soul with pleasure, and she looked aside on him happy and well-content.

O they crossed the stream by the shallow below the pool wherein Walter had bathed, & within a little they came upon a tall fence of flake-hurdles, and a simple gate therein. The Lady opened the same, and they entered thereby into a close all

85

planted as a most fair garden, with hedges of rose and woodbine, and with linden-trees a-blossom, & long ways of green grass betwixt borders of lilies and clove-giliflowers, and other sweet garland-flowers. And a branch of the stream which they had crossed erewhile wandered through that garden; and in the midst was a little house built of post & pan, and thatched with yellow straw, as if it were new done.

THEN Walter looked this way and that, & wondered at first, & tried to think in his mind what should come next, and how matters would go with him; but his thought would not dwell steady on any other matter than the beauty of the Lady amidst the beauty of the garden; & withal she was now grown so sweet and kind, & even somewhat timid & shy with him, that scarce did he know whose hand he held, or whose fragrant bosom and sleek side went so close to him.

So they wandered here and there through the waning of the day, and when they entered at last into the cool dusk house, then they loved & played together, as if they were a pair of lovers guileless, with no fear for the morrow, and no seeds of enmity and death sown betwixt them.

CHAPTER XVIII ⁄ THE MAID GIVES WALTER TRYST

OW on the morrow, when Walter was awake, he found there was no one lying beside him, and the day was no longer very young; so he arose, and went through the garden from end to end, and all about, and there was none there, & albeit that he dreaded to meet the Lady there, yet was he sad at heart & fearful of what might betide. Howsoever, he found the gate whereby they had entered yesterday, and he went out into the little dale; but when he had gone a step or two he turned about, & could see neither garden nor fence, nor any sign of what he had seen thereof but lately. He knit his brow and stood still to think of it, & his heart grew the heavier thereby; but presently he went his ways and crossed the stream, but had scarce come up on to the grass on the further side, ere he saw a woman coming to meet him, and at first, full as he was of the tide of yesterday and the wondrous garden, deemed that it would be the Lady; but the woman stayed her feet, and, stooping, laid a hand on her right ankle, & he saw that it was the Maid. He drew anigh to her, and saw that she was nought so sad of counten⁄ance as the last time she had met him, but flushed of cheek & bright⁄eyed.

As he came up to her she made a step or two to meet him, holding out her two hands, and then refrained her, & said smiling: Ah, friend, belike this shall be the last time that I shall say to thee, touch me not, nay, not so much as my hand, or if it were but the hem of my raiment.

The joy grew up in his heart, and he gazed on her fondly, and said: Why, what then hath befallen of late?

O friend, she began, this hath befallen.

But as he looked on her, the smile died from her face, & she became deadly pale to the very lips; she looked askance to her left side, whereas ran the stream; and Walter followed her eyes, and deemed for one instant that he saw the misshapen yellow visage of the dwarf peering round from a grey rock, but the next there was nothing. Then the Maid, though she were as pale as death, went on in a clear, steady, hard voice, wherein was no joy or kindness, keeping her face to Walter & her back to the stream: This hath befallen, friend, that there is no longer any need to refrain thy love nor mine; therefore I say to thee, come to my chamber (& it is the red chamber over against thine, though thou knewest it not) an hour before this next midnight, & then thy sorrow and mine shall be at an end: and now I must needs depart. Follow me not, but remember!

And therewith she turned about & fled like the wind down the stream.

BUT Walter stood wondering, and knew not what to make of it, whether it were for good or ill: for he knew now that she had paled & been seized with terror because of the up-heaving of the ugly head; & yet she had seemed to speak out the very thing she had to say. Howsoever it were, he spake aloud to himself: Whatever comes, I will keep tryst with her.

Then he drew his sword, and turned this way & that, looking all about if he might see any sign of the Evil Thing; but nought might his eyes behold, save the grass, and the stream, and the bushes of the dale. So then, still holding his naked sword in his hand, he clomb the bent out of the dale; for that was the only way he knew to the Golden House; and when he came to the top, & the summer breeze blew in his face, and he looked down a fair green slope beset with goodly oaks and chestnuts, he was refreshed with the life of the earth, and he felt the good sword in his fist, and knew that there was might and longing in him, & the world seemed open unto him.

So he smiled, if it were somewhat grimly, and sheathed his sword and went on toward the house.

CHAPTER XIX ⁄ WALTER GOES TO FETCH HOME THE LION'S HIDE

E entered the cool dusk through the porch, and, looking down the pillared hall, saw beyond the fountain a gleam of gold, and when he came past the said fountain he looked up to the high⁄seat, and lo! the Lady sitting there clad in her queenly raiment. She called to him, and he came; and she hailed him, and spake graciously and calmly, yet as if she knew nought of him save as the leal servant of her, a high Lady. Squire, she said, we have deemed it meet to have the hide of the servant of the Enemy, the lion to wit, whom thou slewest yesterday, for a carpet to our

feet; wherefore go now, take thy wood-knife, and flay the beast, and bring me home his skin. This shall be all thy service for this day, so mayst thou do it at thine own leisure, and not weary thyself. May good go with thee.

He bent the knee before her, and she smiled on him graciously, but reached out no hand for him to kiss, and heeded him but little. Wherefore, in spite of himself, and though he knew somewhat of her guile, he could not help marvelling that this should be she who had lain in his arms night-long but of late.

HOWSO that might be, he took his way toward the thicket where he had slain the lion, & came thither by then it was afternoon, at the hottest of the day. So he entered therein, and came to the very place whereas the Lady had lain, when she fell down before the terror of the lion; & there was the mark of her body on the grass where she had lain that while, like as it were the form of a hare. But when Walter went on to where he had slain that great beast, lo! he was gone, and there was no sign of him; but there were Walter's own foot-prints, & the two shafts which he had shot, one feathered red, and one blue. He said at first: Belike someone hath been here, & hath had the carcase away. Then he laughed in very despite, & said: How may that be, since there are no signs of dragging away of so huge a body, and no blood or fur on the grass if they had cut him up, & moreover no trampling of feet, as if there had been many men at the deed. Then was he all abashed, and again laughed in scorn of himself, & said: Forsooth I deemed I had done manly; but now forsooth I shot nought, & nought there was before the sword of my father's son. And what may I deem now, but that this is a land of mere lies, & that there is nought real and alive therein save me. Yea, belike even these trees & the green grass will presently depart from me, & leave me falling down through the clouds.

Therewith he turned away, & gat him to the road that led to the Golden House, wondering what next should befall him, and going slowly as he pondered his case. So came he to that first thicket where they had lost their quarry by water; so he entered the same, musing, and bathed him in the pool that was therein, after he had wandered about it a while, and found nothing new.

So again he set him to the homeward road, when the day was now waning, and it was near sunset that he was come nigh unto the house, though it was hidden from him as then by a low bent that rose before him; & there he abode and looked about him.

NOW as he looked, over the said bent came the figure of a woman, who stayed on the brow thereof and looked all about her, and then ran swiftly down to meet Walter, who saw at once that it was the Maid.

She made no stay then till she was but three paces from him, and then she stooped down and made the sign to him, & then spake to him breathlessly, and said: Hearken! but speak not till I have done: I bade thee to-night's meeting because I saw that there was one anigh whom I must needs beguile. But by thine oath, and thy love, and all that thou art, I adjure thee come not unto me this night as I bade thee! but be hidden in the hazel-copse outside the house, as it draws toward midnight, & abide me there. Dost thou hearken, and wilt thou? Say yes or no in haste, for I may not tarry a moment of time. Who knoweth what is behind me.

Yes, said Walter hastily; but friend and love . . .

No more, she said; hope the best; and turning from him she ran away swiftly, not by the way she had come, but sideways, as though to reach the house by fetching a compass.

BUT Walter went slowly on his way, thinking within himself that now at that present moment there was nought for it but to refrain him from doing, and to let others do; yet deemed he that it was little manly to be as the pawn upon the board, pushed about by the will of others.

Then, as he went, he bethought him of the Maiden's face & aspect, as she came running to him, and stood before him for that minute; and all eagerness he saw in her, and sore love of him, & distress of soul, all blent together.

SO came he to the brow of the bent, whence he could see lying before him, scarce more than a bow-shot away, the Golden House, now gilded again and reddened by the setting sun. And even therewith came a gay image toward him, flashing back the level rays from gold and steel and silver; and lo! there was come the King's Son. They met presently, & the King's Son turned to go beside him, & said merrily: I give thee good even, my Lady's Squire! I owe thee something of courtesy, whereas it is by thy means that I shall be made happy, both to-night, and to-morrow, and many to-morrows; and sooth it is, that but little courtesy have I done thee hitherto.

His face was full of joy, and the eyes of him shone

with gladness. He was a goodly man, but to Walter he seemed an ill one; and he hated him so much, that he found it no easy matter to answer him; but he refrained himself, and said: I can thee thank, King's Son; and good it is that someone is happy in this strange land.

Art thou not happy then, Squire of my Lady? said the other.

Walter had no mind to show this man his heart, nay, nor even a corner thereof; for he deemed him an enemy. So he smiled sweetly & somewhat foolishly, as a man luckily in love, & said: O yea, yea, why should I not be so? How might I be otherwise?

Yea then, said the King's Son, why didst thou say that thou wert glad someone is happy? Who is unhappy deemest thou? and he looked on him keenly.

Walter answered slowly: Said I so? I suppose then that I was thinking of thee; for when first I saw thee, yea, and afterwards, thou didst seem heavy-hearted and ill-content.

The face of the King's Son cleared at this word, & he said: Yea, so it was; for look you, both ways it was: I was unfree, and I had sown the true desire of my heart whereas it waxed not. But now I am on the brink and verge of freedom, & presently shall my desire be blossomed. Nay now, Squire, I deem thee a good fellow, though it may be somewhat of a fool; so I will no more speak riddles to thee. Thus it is: the Maid hath promised me all mine asking, and is mine; and in two or three days, by her helping also, I shall see the world again.

Quoth Walter, smiling askance on him: And the Lady? what shall she say to this matter?

The King's Son reddened, but smiled falsely enough,

and said: Sir Squire, thou knowest enough not to need to ask this. Why should I tell thee that she accounteth more of thy little finger than of my whole body? Now I tell thee hereof freely; first, because this my fruition of love, and my freeing from thralldom, is, in a way, of thy doing. For thou art become my supplanter, and hast taken thy place with yonder lovely tyrant. Fear not for me! she will let me go. As for thyself, see thou to it! But again I tell thee hereof because my heart is light and full of joy, and telling thee will pleasure me, & cannot do me any harm. For if thou say: How if I carry the tale to my Lady? I answer, thou wilt not. For I know that thine heart hath been somewhat set on the jewel that my hand holdeth; & thou knowest well on whose head the Lady's wrath would fall, & that would be neither thine nor mine.

Thou sayest sooth, said Walter; neither is treason my wont.

SO they walked on silently a while, and then Walter said: But how if the Maiden had nay-said thee; what hadst thou done then?

By the heavens! said the King's Son fiercely, she should have paid for her nay-say; then would I . . . But he broke off, & said quietly, yet somewhat doggedly: Why talk of what might have been? She gave me her yea-say pleasantly and sweetly.

Now Walter knew that the man lied, so he held his peace thereon; but presently he said: When thou art free wilt thou go to thine own land again?

Yea, said the King's Son; she will lead me thither.

And wilt thou make her thy lady and queen when thou comest to thy father's land? said Walter.

The King's Son knit his brow, and said: When I am in mine own land I may do with her what I will; but I look for it that I shall do no otherwise with her than that she shall be well-content.

THEN the talk between them dropped, and the King's Son turned off toward the wood, singing & joyous; but Walter went soberly toward the house. Forsooth, he was not greatly cast down, for besides that he knew that the King's Son was false, he deemed that under this double tryst lay something which was a-doing in his own behalf. Yet was he eager and troubled, if not down-hearted, and his soul was cast about betwixt hope and fear.

CHAPTER XX · WALTER IS BIDDEN TO ANOTHER TRYST

SO came he into the pillared hall, & there he found the Lady walking to and fro by the high-seat; & when he drew nigh she turned on him, & said in a voice rather eager than angry: What hast thou done, Squire? Why art thou come before me?

He was abashed, and bowed before her and said: O gracious Lady, thou badest me service, & I have been about it.

She said: Tell me then, tell me, what hath betided?

Lady, said he, when I entered the thicket of thy swooning I found there no carcase of the lion, nor any sign of the dragging away of him.

She looked full in his face for a little, and then went

95

to her chair, and sat down therein; and in a little while spake to him in a softer voice, and said: Did I not tell thee that some enemy had done that unto me? & lo! now thou seest that so it is.

Then was she silent again, and knit her brows and set her teeth; and thereafter she spake harshly & fiercely: But I will overcome her, & make her days evil, but keep death away from her, that she may die many times over; and know all the sickness of the heart, when foes be nigh, and friends afar, & there is none to deliver!

Her eyes flashed, and her face was dark with anger; but she turned and caught Walter's eyes, & the sternness of his face, and she softened at once, & said: But thou! this hath little to do with thee; and now to thee I speak: Now cometh even and night. Go thou to thy chamber, and there shalt thou find raiment worthy of thee, what thou now art, and what thou shalt be; do on the same, & make thyself most goodly, and then come thou hither & eat and drink with me, & afterwards depart whither thou wilt, till the night has worn to its mid-most; & then come thou to my chamber, to wit, through the ivory door in the gallery above; and then and there shall I tell thee a thing, and it shall be for the weal both of thee & of me, but for the grief and woe of the Enemy.

Therewith she reached her hand to him, and he kissed it, and departed & came to his chamber, & found raiment there before rich beyond measure; & he wondered if any new snare lay therein: yet if there were, he saw no way whereby he might escape it, so he did it on, and became as the most glorious of kings, & yet lovelier than any king of the world.

SITHENCE he went his way into the pillared hall, when it was now night, & without the moon was up, & the trees of the wood as still as images. But within the hall shone bright with many candles, & the fountain glittered in the light of them, as it ran tinkling sweetly into the little stream; & the silvern bridges gleamed, and the pillars shone all round about.

And there on the dais was a table dight most royally, and the Lady sitting thereat, clad in her most glorious array, & behind her the Maid standing humbly, yet clad in precious web of shimmering gold, but with feet unshod, and the iron ring upon her ankle.

SO Walter came his ways to the high-seat, and the Lady rose and greeted him, and took him by the hands, and kissed him on either cheek, & sat him down beside her. So they fell to their meat, & the Maid served them; but the Lady took no more heed of her than if she were one of the pillars of the hall; but Walter she caressed oft with sweet words, & the touch of her hand, making him drink out of her cup and eat out of her dish. As to him, he was bashful by seeming, but verily fearful; he took the Lady's caresses with what grace he might, & durst not so much as glance at her Maid. Long indeed seemed that banquet to him, and longer yet endured the weariness of his abiding there, kind to his foe and unkind to his friend; for after the banquet they still sat a while, & the Lady talked much to Walter about many things of the ways of the world, and he answered what he might, distraught as he was with the thought of those two trysts which he had to deal with.

T last spake the Lady and said: Now must I leave thee for a little, and thou wottest where and how we shall meet next; and meanwhile disport thee as thou wilt, so that thou weary not thyself, for I love to see thee joyous.

Then she arose stately and grand; but she kissed Walter on the mouth ere she turned to go out of the hall. The Maid followed her; but or ever she was quite gone, she stooped and made that sign, and looked over her shoulder at Walter, as if in entreaty to him, & there was fear & anguish in her face; but he nodded his head to her in yea-say of the tryst in the hazel-copse, and in a trice she was gone.

ALTER went down the hall, and forth into the early night; but in the jaws of the porch he came up against the King's Son, who, gazing at his attire glittering with all its gems in the moonlight, laughed out, and said: Now may it be seen how thou art risen in degree above me, whereas I am but a king's son, and that a king of a far country; whereas thou art a king of kings, or shalt be this night, yea, and of this very country wherein we both are.

Now Walter saw the mock which lay under his words; but he kept back his wrath, and answered: Fair sir, art thou as well contented with thy lot as when the sun went down? Hast thou no doubt or fear? Will the Maid verily keep tryst with thee, or hath she given thee yea-say but to escape thee this time? Or, again, may she not turn to the Lady & appeal to her against thee?

Now when he had spoken these words, he repented thereof, & feared for himself and the Maid, lest he had stirred some misgiving in that young man's foolish heart. But the King's Son did but laugh, & answered nought but to Walter's last words, & said: Yea, yea! this word of thine showeth how little thou wottest of that which lieth betwixt my darling and thine. Doth the lamb appeal from the shepherd to the wolf? Even so shall the Maid appeal from me to thy Lady. What! ask thy Lady at thy leisure what her wont hath been with her thrall; she shall think it a fair tale to tell thee thereof. But thereof is my Maid all whole now by reason of her wisdom in leechcraft, or somewhat more. And now I tell thee again, that the beforesaid Maid must needs do my will; for if I be the deep sea, & I deem not so ill of myself, that other one is the devil; as belike thou shalt find out for thyself later on. Yea, all is well with me, and more than well.

And therewith he swung merrily into the litten hall. But Walter went out into the moonlit night, and wandered about for an hour or more, and stole warily into the hall & thence into his own chamber. There he did off that royal array, & did his own raiment upon him; he girt him with sword & knife, took his bow and quiver, and stole down and out again, even as he had come in. Then he fetched a compass, and came down into that hazel coppice from the north, and lay all hidden there while the night wore, till he deemed it would lack but little of midnight.

CHAPTER XXI · WALTER AND THE MAID FLEE FROM THE GOLDEN HOUSE

HERE he abode amidst the hazels, harkening every littlest sound; & the sounds were nought but the night voices of the wood, till suddenly there burst forth from the house a great wailing cry. Walter's heart came up into his mouth, but he had no time to do aught, for following hard on the cry came the sound of light feet close to him, the boughs were thrust aside, & there was come the Maid, and she but in her white coat, & barefoot. And then first he felt the sweetness of her flesh on his, for she caught him by the hand & said breathlessly: Now, now! there may yet be time, or even too much, it may be. For the saving of breath ask me no questions, but come!

He dallied not, but went as she led, and they were light-foot, both of them.

HEY went the same way, due south to wit, whereby he had gone a-hunting with the Lady; and whiles they ran & whiles they walked; but so fast they went, that by grey of the dawn they were come as far as that coppice or thicket of the Lion; & still they hastened onward, & but little had the Maid spoken, save here & there a word to hearten up Walter, and here & there a shy word of endear-ment. At last the dawn grew into early day, & as they came over the brow of a bent, they looked down over a plain land whereas the trees grew scatter-meal, & beyond the plain rose up the land into long green hills, and over those again were blue mountains great and far away.

Then spake the Maid: Over yonder lie the outlying mountains of the Bears, & through them we needs must pass, to our great peril.

Nay, friend, she said, as he handled his sword-hilt, it must be patience and wisdom to bring us through, and not the fallow blade of one man, though he be a good one. But look! below there runs a stream through the first of the plain, and I see nought for it but we must now rest our bodies. Moreover I have a tale to tell thee which is burning my heart; for maybe there will be a pardon to ask of thee moreover; wherefore I fear thee.

Quoth Walter: How may that be?

She answered him not, but took his hand and led him down the bent. But he said: Thou sayest, rest; but are we now out of all peril of the chase?

She said: I cannot tell till I know what hath befallen her. If she be not to hand to set on her trackers, they will scarce happen on us now; if it be not for that one.

And she shuddered, and he felt her hand change as he held it.

Then she said: But peril or no peril, needs must we rest; for I tell thee again, what I have to say to thee burneth my bosom for fear of thee, so that I can go no further until I have told thee.

Then he said: I wot not of this Queen & her mightiness & her servants. I will ask thereof later. But besides the others, is there not the King's Son, he who loves thee so unworthily?

She paled somewhat, and said: As for him, there had been nought for thee to fear in him, save his treason: but now shall he neither love nor hate any more; he died last midnight.

Yea, & how? said Walter.

Nay, she said, let me tell my tale all together once for all, lest thou blame me overmuch. But first we will wash us and comfort us as best we may, and then amidst our resting shall the word be said.

BY then were they come down to the stream-side, which ran fair in pools and stickles amidst rocks & sandy banks. She said: There behind the great grey rock is my bath, friend; and here is thine; and lo! the uprising of the sun!

So she went her ways to the said rock, & he bathed him, and washed the night off him, and by then he was clad again she came back fresh and sweet from the water, & with her lap full of cherries from a wilding which overhung her bath. So they sat down together on the green grass above the sand, & ate the breakfast of the wilderness: and Walter was full of content as he watched her, and beheld her sweetness and her loveliness; yet were they, either of them, somewhat shy & shamefaced each with the other; so that he did but kiss her hands once & again, and though she shrank not from him, yet had she no boldness to cast herself into his arms.

CHAPTER XXII ⁄ OF THE DWARF AND THE PARDON

OW she began to say: My friend, now shall I tell thee what I have done for thee and me; and if thou have a mind to blame me, & punish me, yet remember first, that what I have done has been for thee & our hope of happy life. Well, I shall tell thee . . .

But therewithal her speech failed her; and, springing up, she faced the bent and pointed with her finger, & she all deadly pale, & shaking so that she might scarce stand, & might speak no word, though a feeble gibbering came from her mouth.

ALTER leapt up and put his arm about her, & looked whitherward she pointed, and at first saw nought; and then nought but a brown and yellow rock rolling down the bent: & then at last he saw that it was the Evil Thing which had met him when first he came into that land; and now it stood upright, and he could see that it was clad in a coat of yellow samite.

Then Walter stooped down and gat his bow into his hand, and stood before the Maid, while he nocked an arrow. But the monster made ready his tackle while Walter was stooping down, & or ever he could loose, his bow⁄string twanged, and an arrow flew forth and grazed the Maid's arm above the elbow, so that the blood ran, and the Dwarf gave forth a harsh & horrible cry. Then flew Walter's shaft, & true was it aimed, so that it smote the monster full on the breast, but fell down from him as if he were made of stone.

Then the creature set up his horrible cry again, and loosed withal, and Walter deemed that he had smitten the Maid, for she fell down in a heap behind him. Then waxed Walter wood-wroth, and cast down his bow and drew his sword, and strode forward towards the bent against the Dwarf. But he roared out again, and there were words in his roar, & he said: Fool! thou shalt go free if thou wilt give up the Enemy.

And who, said Walter, is the Enemy?

Yelled the Dwarf: She, the pink & white thing lying there; she is not dead yet; she is but dying for fear of me. Yea, she hath reason! I could have set the shaft in her heart as easily as scratching her arm; but I need her body alive, that I may wreak me on her.

What wilt thou do with her? said Walter; for now he had heard that the Maid was not slain he had waxed wary again, & stood watching his chance.

The Dwarf yelled so at his last word, that no word came from the noise a while, & then he said: What will I with her? Let me at her, and stand by & look on, and then shalt thou have a strange tale to carry off with thee. For I will let thee go this while.

Said Walter: But what need to wreak thee? What hath she done to thee?

What need! what need! roared the Dwarf; have I not told thee that she is the Enemy? And thou askest of what she hath done! of what! fool, she is the murderer! she hath slain the Lady that was our Lady, and that made us; she whom all we worshipped and adored. O impudent fool!

Therewith he nocked & loosed another arrow, which would have smitten Walter in the face, but that he lowered his head in the very nick of time; then with a great shout he rushed up the bent, and was on the Dwarf before he could get his sword out, and leaping aloft dealt the creature a stroke amid⁄most of the crown; and so mightily he smote, that he drave the heavy sword right through to the teeth, so that he fell dead straightway.

ALTER stood over him a minute, and when he saw that he moved not, he went slowly down to the stream, whereby the Maid yet lay cowering down and quivering all over, & covering her face with her hands. Then he took her by the wrist & said: Up Maiden, up! and tell me this tale of the slaying!

But she shrunk away from him, and looked at him with wild eyes, and said: What hast thou done with him? Is he gone?

He is dead, said Walter; I have slain him; there lies he with cloven skull on the bent⁄side: unless, forsooth, he vanish away like the lion I slew! or else, perchance, he will come to life again! And art thou a lie like to the rest of them? let me hear of this slaying.

HE rose up, & stood before him trembling, and said: O, thou art angry with me, and thine anger I cannot bear. Ah, what have I done? Thou hast slain one, and I, maybe, the other; & never had we escaped till both these twain were dead. Ah! thou dost not know! thou dost not know! O me! what shall I do to appease thy wrath!

E looked on her, & his heart rose to his mouth at the thought of sundering from her. Still he looked on her, and her piteous friendly face melted all his heart; he threw down his sword, and took her by the shoulders, and kissed her face over and over, and strained her to him, so that he felt the sweet, ness of her bosom. Then he lifted her up like a child, and set her down on the green grass, and went down to the water, and filled his hat therefrom, and came back to her; then he gave her to drink, and bathed her face and her hands, so that the colour came aback to the cheeks and lips of her: and she smiled on him, & kissed his hands, and said: O now thou art kind to me.

Yea, said he, and true it is that if thou hast slain, I have done no less, and if thou hast lied, even so have I; & if thou hast played the wanton, as I deem not that thou hast, I full surely have so done. So now thou shalt pardon me, & when thy spirit has come back to thee, thou shalt tell me thy tale in all friendship, and in all loving-kindness will I hearken the same.

THEREWITH he knelt before her & kissed her feet. But she said: Yea, yea; what thou willest, that will I do. But first tell me one thing. Hast thou buried this horror & hidden him in the earth?

He deemed that fear had bewildered her, and that she scarcely yet knew how things had gone. But he said: Fair sweet friend, I have not done it as yet; but now will I go and do it, if it seem good to thee.

Yea, she said, but first must thou smite off his head, and lay it by his buttocks when he is in the earth; or evil things will happen else. This of the burying is no idle matter, I bid thee believe.

I doubt it not, said he; surely such malice as was in this one will be hard to slay. And he picked up his sword, and turned to go to the field of deed.

She said: I must needs go with thee; terror hath so

filled my soul, that I durst not abide here without thee.

SO they went both together to where the creature lay. The Maid durst not look on the dead monster, but Walter noted that he was girt with a big ungainly sax; so he drew it from the sheath, and there smote off the hideous head of the fiend with his own weapon. Then they twain together laboured the earth, she with Walter's sword, he with the ugly sax, till they had made a grave deep & wide enough; and therein they thrust the creature, and covered him up, weapons and all together.

CHAPTER XXIII ⁄ OF THE PEACEFUL ENDING OF THAT WILD DAY

THEREAFTER Walter led the Maid down again, & said to her: Now, sweetling, shall the story be told.

Nay friend, she said, not here. This place hath been polluted by my craven fear, and the horror of the vile wretch, of whom no words may tell his vileness. Let us hence and onward. Thou seest I have once more come to life again.

But, said he, thou hast been hurt by the Dwarf's arrow.

She laughed, and said: Had I never had greater hurt from them than that, little had been the tale thereof: yet whereas thou lookest dolorous about it, we will speedily heal it.

Therewith she sought about, & found nigh the

stream‑side certain herbs; and she spake words over them, and bade Walter lay them on the wound, which, forsooth, was of the least, and he did so, and bound a strip of his shirt about her arm; and then would she set forth. But he said: Thou art all unshod; and but if that be seen to, our journey shall be stayed by thy foot‑soreness: I may make a shift to fashion thee brogues.

She said: I may well go barefoot. And in any case, I entreat thee that we tarry here no longer, but go away hence, if it be but for a mile.

And she looked piteously on him, so that he might not gainsay her.

S O then they crossed the stream, and set forward, when amidst all these haps the day was worn to mid‑morning. But after they had gone a mile, they sat them down on a knoll under the shadow of a big thorn‑tree, within sight of the mountains. Then said Walter: Now will I cut thee the brogues from the skirt of my buff‑coat, which shall be well meet for such work; and meanwhile shalt thou tell me thy tale.

Thou art kind, she said; but be kinder yet, & abide my tale till we have done our day's work. For we were best to make no long delay here; because, though thou hast slain the King‑dwarf, yet there be others of his kindred, who swarm in some parts of the wood as the rabbits in a warren. Now true it is that they have but little understanding, less, it may be, than the very brute beasts; and that, as I said afore, unless they be set on our slot like to hounds, they shall have no inkling of where to seek us, yet might they happen upon us by mere misadventure. And moreover friend, quoth she, blushing, I would beg of thee some little respite; for though I scarce fear thy wrath any more, since thou hast been so kind to me, yet is there shame in that which I have to tell thee. Wherefore since the fairest of the day is before us, let us use it all we may, and, when thou hast done me my new foot-gear, get us gone forward again.

HE kissed her kindly and yea-said her asking: he had already fallen to work on the leather, and in a while had fashioned her the brogues; so she tied them to her feet, and arose with a smile & said: Now am I hale and strong again, what with the rest, and what with thy loving-kindness, & thou shalt see how nimble I shall be to leave this land, for as fair as it is. Since forsooth a land of lies it is, and of grief to the children of Adam.

SO they went their ways thence, & fared nimbly indeed, & made no stay till some three hours after noon, when they rested by a thicket-side, where the strawberries grew plenty; they ate thereof what they would: & from a great oak hard by Walter shot him first one culver, and then another, & hung them to his girdle to be for their evening's meat; sithence they went forward again, and nought befell them to tell of, till they were come, whenas it lacked scarce an hour of sunset, to the banks of another river, not right great, but bigger than the last one. There the Maid cast herself down & said: Friend, no further will thy friend go this even; nay, to say sooth, she cannot. So now we will eat of thy venison, & then shall my tale be, since I may no longer delay it; and thereafter shall our slumber be sweet and safe as I deem.

She spake merrily now, and as one who feared nothing, and Walter was much heartened by her words and her voice, and he fell to and made a fire, and a woodland oven in the earth, and sithence dighted his fowl, & baked them after the manner of woodmen. And they ate, both of them, in all love, & in good-liking of life, and were much strengthened by their supper. And when they were done, Walter eked his fire, both against the chill of the midnight and dawning, and for a guard against wild beasts, and by that time night was come, and the moon arisen. Then the Maiden drew up to the fire, and turned to Walter and spake.

CHAPTER XXIV - THE MAID TELLS OF WHAT HAD BEFALLEN HER

OW, friend, by the clear of the moon & this firelight will I tell what I may and can of my tale. Thus it is: If I be wholly of the race of Adam I wot not; nor can I tell thee how many years old I may be. For there are, as it were, shards or gaps in my life, wherein are but a few things dimly remembered, and doubtless many things forgotten. I remember well when I was a little child, and right happy, & there were people about me whom I loved, and who loved me. It was not in this land; but all things were lovely there; the year's beginning, the happy mid-year, the year's waning, the year's ending, & then again its beginning. That passed away, and then for a while is more than dimness, for nought I remember save that I was. Thereafter I remember again, & am a young

maiden, and I know some things, and long to know more. I am nowise happy; I am amongst people who bid me go, and I go; and do this, & I do it: none loveth me, none tormenteth me; but I wear my heart in longing for I scarce know what. Neither then am I in this land, but in a land that I love not, and a house that is big & stately, but nought lovely. Then is a dim time again, and sithence a time not right clear; an evil time, wherein I am older, well-nigh grown to womanhood. There are a many folk about me, and they foul, and greedy, and hard; & my spirit is fierce, but my body feeble; and I am set to tasks that I would not do, by them that are unwiser than I; & smitten I am by them that are less valiant than I; and I know lack, & stripes, and divers misery. But all that is now become but a dim picture to me, save that amongst all these unfriends is a friend to me; an old woman, who telleth me sweet tales of other life, wherein all is high & goodly, or at the least valiant and doughty, & she setteth hope in my heart and learneth me, & maketh me to know much . . . O much . . . so that at last I am grown wise, and wise to be mighty if I durst. Yet am I nought in this land all this while, but, as meseemeth, in a great and a foul city.

AND then, as it were, I fall asleep; and in my sleep is nought, save here & there a wild dream, somedeal lovely, somedeal hideous: but of this dream is my Mistress a part, and the monster, withal, whose head thou didst cleave to-day. But when I am awaken from it, then am I verily in this land, and myself, as thou seest me to-day. And the first part of my life here is this, that I am in the pillared hall yonder, half-clad & with bound hands; and the Dwarf leadeth me to the Lady, and I hear his horrible croak as he sayeth: Lady, will this one do? & then the sweet voice of the Lady saying: This one will do; thou shalt have thy reward: now, set thou the token upon her. Then I remember the Dwarf dragging me away, and my heart sinking for fear of him; but for that time he did me no more harm than the rivetting upon my leg this iron ring which here thou seest.

SO from that time forward I have lived in this land, & been the thrall of the Lady; & I remember my life here day by day, & no part of it has fallen into the dimness of dreams. Thereof will I tell thee but little: but this I will tell thee, that in spite of my past dreams, or it may be because of them, I had not lost the wisdom which the old woman had erst learned me, & for more wisdom I longed. Maybe this longing shall now make both thee & me happy, but for the passing time it brought me grief. For at first my Mistress was indeed wayward with me, but as any great lady might be with her bought thrall, whiles caressing me, and whiles chastising me, as her mood went; but she seemed not to be cruel of malice, or with any set purpose. But so it was (rather little by little than by any great sudden uncovering of my intent), that she came to know that I also had some of the wisdom whereby she lived her queenly life. That was about two years after I was first her thrall, and three weary years have gone by since she began to see in me the enemy of her days. Now why or wherefore I know not, but it seemeth that it would not avail her to slay me outright, or suffer me to die; but nought with-held her from piling up griefs and miseries on my head. At last she set her servant, the Dwarf, upon me, even

112

he whose head thou clavest to-day. Many things I bore from him whereof it were unseemly for my tongue to tell before thee; but the time came when he exceeded, and I could bear no more; and then I showed him this sharp knife (wherewith I would have thrust me through to the heart if thou hadst not pardoned me e'en now), & I told him that if he forbore me not, I would slay, not him, but myself; and this he might not away with because of the commandment of the Lady, who had given him the word that in any case I must be kept living. And her hand, withal, fear held somewhat hereafter. Yet was there need to me of all my wisdom; for with all this her hatred grew, & whiles raged within her so furiously that it overmastered her fear, & at such times she would have put me to death if I had not escaped her by some turn of my lore.

OW further, I shall tell thee that somewhat more than a year ago hither to this land came the King's Son, the second goodly man, as thou art the third, whom her sorceries have drawn hither since I have dwelt here. Forsooth, when he first came, he seemed to us, to me, & yet more to my Lady, to be as beautiful as an angel, and sorely she loved him; & he her, after his fashion: but he was light-minded, and cold-hearted, and in a while he must needs turn his eyes upon me, and offer me his love, which was but foul and unkind as it turned out; for when I nay-said him, as maybe I had not done save for fear of my Mistress, he had no pity upon me, but spared not to lead me into the trap of her wrath, and leave me without help, or a good word. But, O friend, in spite of all grief and anguish, I learned still, and waxed wise, and wiser, abiding the day of my deliverance, which has come, and thou art come.

HEREWITH she took Walter's hands and kissed them; but he kissed her face, & her tears wet his lips. Then she went on: But sithence, months ago, the Lady began to weary of this dastard, despite of his beauty; & then it was thy turn to be swept into her net; I partly guess how. For on a day in broad daylight, as I was serving my Mistress in the hall, and the Evil Thing, whose head is now cloven, was lying across the threshold of the door, as it were a dream fell upon me, though I strove to cast it off for fear of chastisement; for the pillared hall wavered, and vanished from my sight, and my feet were treading a rough stone pavement instead of the marble wonder of the hall, and there was the scent of the salt sea and of the tackle of ships, and behind me were tall houses, and before me the ships indeed, with their ropes beating and their sails flapping & their masts wavering; and in mine ears was the hale and how of mariners; things that I had seen and heard in the dimness of my life gone by.

And there was I, & the Dwarf before me, and the Lady after me, going over the gangway aboard of a tall ship, and she gathered way and was gotten out of the haven, & straightway I saw the mariners cast abroad their ancient.

Quoth Walter: What then! Sawest thou the blazon thereon, of a wolf-like beast ramping up against a maiden? And that might well have been thou.

She said: Yea, so it was; but refrain thee, that I may tell on my tale! The ship and the sea vanished away, but I was not back in the hall of the Golden House; & again were we three in the street of the self-same town which we had but just left; but somewhat dim was my vision thereof, and I saw little save the door of a goodly house before me, and speedily it died out, and we were again in the pillared hall, wherein my thralldom was made manifest.

MAIDEN, said Walter, one question I would ask thee; to wit, didst thou see me on the quay by the ships?

Nay, she said, there were many folk about, but they were all as images of the aliens to me. Now hearken further: three months thereafter came the dream upon me again, when we were all three together in the Pillared Hall; & again was the vision somewhat dim. Once more we were in the street of a busy town, but all unlike to that other one, and there were men standing together on our right hands by the door of a house.

Yea, yea, quoth Walter; and, forsooth, one of them was who but I.

Refrain thee, beloved! she said; for my tale draweth to its ending, & I would have thee hearken heedfully: for maybe thou shalt once again deem my deed past pardon. Some twenty days after this last dream, I had some leisure from my Mistress's service, so I went to disport me by the Well of the Oak-tree (or forsooth she might have set in my mind the thought of going there, that I might meet thee and give her some occasion against me); & I sat thereby, nowise loving the earth, but sick at heart, because of late the King's Son had been more than ever instant with me to yield him my body, threatening me else with casting me into all that the worst could do to me of torments and shames day by day. I say my heart failed me, & I was well-nigh brought to the point of yea-saying his desires, that I might take the chance of something befalling me that were less bad than the worst. But here must I tell thee a thing, and pray thee to take it to heart. This, more than aught else, had given me strength to nay-say that dast-ard, that my wisdom both hath been, & now is, the wisdom of a wise maid, & not of a woman, and all the might thereof shall I lose with my maidenhead. Evil wilt thou think of me then, for all I was tried so sore, that I was at point to cast it all away, so wretchedly as I shrank from the horror of the Lady's wrath.

BUT thereas I sat pondering these things, I saw a man coming, and thought no otherwise there-of but that it was the King's Son, till I saw the stranger drawing near, & his golden hair, and his grey eyes; & then I heard his voice, and his kindness pierced my heart, and I knew that my friend had come to see me; and O, friend, these tears are for the sweetness of that past hour!

SAID Walter: I came to see my friend, I also. Now have I noted what thou badest me; and I will forbear all as thou commandest me, till we be safe out of the desert & far away from all evil things; but wilt thou ban me from all caresses?

She laughed amidst of her tears, & said: O, nay, poor lad, if thou wilt be but wise.

Then she leaned toward him, & took his face betwixt her hands and kissed him oft, & the tears started in his eyes for love and pity of her.

Then she said: Alas, friend! even yet mayst thou doom me guilty, and all thy love may turn away from me, when I have told thee all that I have done for the sake of thee & me. O, if then there might be some chastisement for the guilty woman, and not mere sundering!

Fear nothing, sweetling, said he; for indeed I deem that already I know partly what thou hast done.

SHE sighed, and said: I will tell thee next, that I banned thy kissing & caressing of me till to-day because I knew that my Mistress would surely know if a man, if thou, hadst so much as touched a finger of mine in love. It was to try me herein that on the morning of the hunting she kissed and embraced me, till I almost died thereof, & showed thee my shoulder & my limbs; & to try thee withal, if thine eye should glister or thy cheek flush thereat; for indeed she was raging in jealousy of thee. Next, my friend, even whiles we were talking together at the Well of the Rock, I was pondering on what we should do to escape from this land of lies. Maybe thou wilt say: Why didst thou not take my hand and flee with me as we fled to-day? Friend, it is most true, that were she not dead we had not escaped thus far. For her trackers would have followed us, set on by her, and brought us back to an evil fate. Therefore I tell thee that from the first I did plot the death of those two, the Dwarf & the Mistress. For no otherwise mightest thou live, or I escape from death in life. But as to the dastard who threatened me with a thrall's pains, I heeded him nought to live or die, for well I knew that thy valiant sword, yea, or thy bare hands, would speedily tame him. Now first I knew that I must make a show of yielding to the King's Son; & somewhat how I did therein, thou knowest. But no night & no time did I give him to bed me, till after I had met thee as thou wentest to the Golden House, before the adventure of fetching the lion's skin; and up to that time I had scarce known what to do, save ever to bid thee, with sore grief and pain, to yield thee to the wicked woman's desire. But as we spake together there by the stream, and I saw that the Evil Thing (whose head thou clavest e'en now) was spying on us, then amidst the sickness of terror which ever came over me whensoever I thought of him, and much more when I saw him (ah! he is dead now!), it came flashing into my mind how I might destroy my enemy. Therefore I made the Dwarf my messenger to her, by bidding thee to my bed in such wise that he might hear it. And wot thou well, that he speedily carried her the tidings. Meanwhile I hastened to lie to the King's Son, and all privily bade him come to me & not thee. And thereafter, by dint of waiting and watching, and taking the only chance that there was, I met thee as thou camest back from fetching the skin of the lion that never was, and gave thee that warning, or else had we been undone indeed.

Said Walter: Was the lion of ·her making or of thine then?

She said: Of hers: why should I deal with such a matter?

Yea, said Walter, but she verily swooned, & she was verily wroth with the Enemy.

The Maid smiled, and said: If her lie was not like very sooth, then had she not been the crafts⁄master that I knew her: one may lie otherwise than with the tongue alone: yet indeed her wrath against the Enemy was nought feigned; for the Enemy was even I, & in these latter days never did her wrath leave me. But to go on with my tale.

Now doubt thou not, that, when thou camest into

the hall yester eve, the Mistress knew of thy counterfeit tryst with me, and meant nought but death for thee; yet first would she have thee in her arms again, therefore did she make much of thee at table (and that was partly for my torment also), and therefore did she make that tryst with thee, and deemed doubtless that thou wouldst not dare to forgo it, even if thou shouldst go to me thereafter.

Now I had trained that dastard to me as I have told thee, but I gave him a sleepy draught, so that when I came to the bed he might not move toward me nor open his eyes: but I lay down beside him, so that the Lady might know that my body had been there; for well had she wotted if it had not. Then as there I lay I cast over him thy shape, so that none might have known, but that thou wert lying by my side, & there, trembling, I abode what should befall. Thus I passed through the hour whenas thou shouldest have been at her chamber, and the time of my tryst with thee was come as the Mistress would be deeming; so that I looked for her speedily, and my heart well-nigh failed me for fear of her cruelty.

Presently then I heard a stirring in her chamber, and I slipped from out the bed, and hid me behind the hangings, and was like to die for fear of her; & lo, presently she came stealing in softly, holding a lamp in one hand and a knife in the other. And I tell thee of a sooth that I also had a sharp knife in my hand to defend my life if need were. She held the lamp up above her head before she drew near to the bed-side, and I heard her mutter: She is not there then! but she shall be taken. Then she went up to the bed and stooped over it, & laid her hand on the place where I had lain;

and therewith her eyes turned to that false image of thee lying there, & she fell a-trembling and shaking, and the lamp fell to the ground & was quenched (but there was bright moonlight in the room, and still I could see what betid). But she uttered a noise like the low roar of a wild beast, and I saw her arm and hand rise up, and the flashing of the steel beneath the hand, and then down came the hand and the steel, and I went nigh to swooning lest perchance I had wrought over well, & thine image were thy very self. The dastard died without a groan: why should I lament him? I cannot. But the Lady drew him toward her, and snatched the clothes from off his shoulders and breast, and fell a-gibbering sounds mostly without meaning, but broken here & there with words. Then I heard her say: I shall forget; I shall forget; & the new days shall come. Then was there silence of her a little, and thereafter she cried out in a terrible voice: O no, no, no! I cannot forget; I cannot forget; & she raised a great wailing cry that filled all the night with horror (didst thou not hear it?), and caught up the knife from the bed and thrust it into her breast, and fell down a dead heap over the bed and on to the man whom she had slain. And then I thought of thee, and joy smote across my terror; how shall I gainsay it? And I fled away to thee, and I took thine hands in mine, thy dear hands, & we fled away together. Shall we be still together?

HE spoke slowly, & touched her not, and she, forbearing all sobbing and weeping, sat looking wistfully on him. He said: I think thou hast told me all; and whether thy guile slew her, or her own evil heart, she was slain last night who lay in mine arms the night before. It was ill, and ill done of

120

me, for I loved not her, but thee, and I wished for her death that I might be with thee. Thou wottest this, and still thou lovest me, it may be overweeningly. What have I to say then? If there be any guilt of guile, I also was in the guile; and if there be any guilt of murder, I also was in the murder. Thus we say to each other; and to God & his Hallows we say: We two have conspired & slain the woman who tormented one of us, & would have slain the other; and if we have done amiss therein, then shall we two together pay the penalty; for in this have we done as one body and one soul.

HEREWITH he put his arms about her and kissed her, but soberly and friendly, as if he would comfort her. And thereafter he said to her: Maybe to-morrow, in the sunlight, I will ask thee of this woman, what she verily was; but now let her be. And thou, thou art over-wearied, and I bid thee sleep.

So he went about and gathered of bracken a great heap for her bed, and did his coat thereover, and led her thereto, & she lay down meekly, and smiled and crossed her arms over her bosom, and presently fell asleep. But as for him, he watched by the fireside till dawn began to glimmer, & then he also laid him down and slept.

HEN the day was bright Walter arose, & met the Maid coming up from the river-bank, fresh & rosy from the water. She paled a little when they met face to face, & she shrank from him shyly. But he took her hand and kissed her frankly; and the two were glad, & had no need to tell each other of their joy, though much else they deemed they had to say, could they have found words thereto.

O they came to their fire and sat down, and fell to breakfast; & ere they were done, the Maid said: My Master, thou seest we be come nigh unto the hill country, and to-day about sunset, belike, we shall come into the Land of the Bear-folk; & both it is, that there is peril if we fall into their hands, and that we may scarce escape them. Yet I deem that we may deal with the peril by wisdom.

What is the peril? said Walter; I mean, what is the worst of it?

Said the Maid: To be offered up in sacrifice to their God.

But if we escape death at their hands, what then? said Walter.

One of two things, said she; the first, that they shall take us into their tribe.

And will they sunder us in that case? said Walter.

Nay, said she.

Walter laughed and said: Therein is little harm then. But what is the other chance?

Said she: That we leave them with their good-will, & come back to one of the lands of Christendom.

Said Walter: I am not all so sure that this is the better of the two choices, though, forsooth, thou seemest to think so. But tell me now, what like is their God, that they should offer up new-comers to him?

Their God is a woman, she said, and the Mother of their nation & tribes (or so they deem) before the days when they had chieftains and Lords of Battle.

That will be long ago, said he; how then may she be living now?

Said the Maid: Doubtless that woman of yore agone is dead this many & many a year; but they take to them still a new woman, one after other, as they may happen on them, to be in the stead of the Ancient Mother. And to tell thee the very truth right out, she that lieth dead in the Pillared Hall has even the last of these; and now, if they knew it, they lack a God. This shall we tell them.

Yea, yea! said Walter, a goodly welcome shall we have of them then, if we come amongst them with our hands red with the blood of their God!

She smiled on him & said: If I come amongst them with the tidings that I have slain her, and they trow therein, without doubt they shall make me Lady & Goddess in her stead.

This is a strange word, said Walter; but if so they do, how shall that further us in reaching the kindreds of the world, and the folk of Holy Church?

HE laughed outright, so joyous was she grown, now that she knew that his life was yet to be a part of hers. Sweetheart, she said, now I see that thou desirest wholly what I desire; yet in any case, abiding with them would be living & not dying, even as thou hadst it e'en now. But, forsooth, they will not hinder our departure if they deem me their God; they do not look for it, nor desire it, that their God should dwell with them daily. Have no fear. Then she laughed again, & said: What! thou lookest on me and deemest me to be but a sorry image of a goddess; & me with my scanty coat and bare arms & naked feet! But wait! I know well how to array me when the time cometh. Thou shalt see it! And now, my Master, were it not meet that we took to the road?

SO they arose, and found a ford of the river that took the Maid but to the knee, and so set forth up the greensward of the slopes whereas there were but few trees; so went they faring toward the hill-country.

At the last they were come to the feet of the very hills, and in the hollows betwixt the buttresses of them grew nut and berry trees, and the greensward round about them was both thick and much flowery. There they stayed them and dined, whereas Walter had shot a hare by the way, and they had found a bubbling spring under a grey stone in a bight of the coppice, wherein now the birds were singing their best.

WHEN they had eaten and had rested some-what, the Maid arose and said: Now shall the Queen array herself, & seem like a very goddess.

Then she fell to work, while Walter looked on; and she made a garland for her head of eglantine where the roses were the fairest; & with mingled flowers of the summer she wreathed her middle about, and let the garland of them hang down to below her knees; and knots of the flowers she made fast to the skirts of her coat, and did them for arm-rings about her arms, and for anklets and sandals for her feet. Then she set a garland about Walter's head, and then stood a little off from him and set her feet together, and lifted up her arms, and said: Lo now! am I not as like to the Mother of Summer as if I were clad in silk and gold? and even so shall I be deemed by the folk of the Bear. Come now, thou shalt see how all shall be well.

HE laughed joyously; but he might scarce laugh for pity of his love. Then they set forth again, and began to climb the hills, and the hours wore as they went in sweet converse; till at last Walter looked on the Maid, and smiled on her, and said: One thing I would say to thee, lovely friend, to wit: wert thou clad in silk & gold, thy stately raiment might well suffer a few stains, or here and there a rent maybe; but stately would it be still when the folk of the Bear should come up against thee. But as to this flowery array of thine, in a few hours it shall be all faded & nought. Nay, even now, as I look on thee, the meadow-sweet that hangeth from thy girdle-stead has waxen dull, & welted; and the blossoming eyebright that is for a hem to the little white coat of thee is already forgetting how to be bright and blue. What sayest thou then?

She laughed at his word, and stood still, and looked back over her shoulder, while with her fingers she dealt with the flowers about her side like to a bird preening his feathers. Then she said: Is it verily so as thou sayest? Look again!

So he looked, & wondered; for lo! beneath his eyes the spires of the meadow-sweet grew crisp & clear again, the eyebright blossoms shone once more over the whiteness of her legs; the eglantine roses opened, and all was as fresh and bright as if it were still growing on its own roots.

HE wondered, & was even somedeal aghast; but she said: Dear friend, be not troubled! did I not tell thee that I am wise in hidden lore? But in my wisdom shall be no longer any scathe to any man. And again, this my wisdom, as I told thee erst, shall end on the day whereon I am made all happy. And it is thou that shall wield it all, my Master. Yet must my wisdom needs endure for a little season yet. Let us on then, boldly and happily.

CHAPTER XXVI ⁄ THEY COME TO THE FOLK OF THE BEARS

O N they went, and before long they were come up on to the down⁄country, where was scarce a tree, save gnarled and knotty thorn⁄bushes here and there, but nought else higher than the whin. And here on these upper lands they saw that the pastures were much burnt with the drought, albeit summer was not worn old. Now they went making due south toward the mountains, whose heads they saw from time to time rising deep blue over the bleak greyness of the downland ridges. And so they went, till at last, hard on sunset, after they had climbed long over a high bent, they came to the brow thereof, &, looking down, beheld new tidings.

There was a wide valley below them, greener than the downs which they had come over, and greener yet amidmost, from the watering of a stream which, all beset with willows, wound about the bottom. Sheep & neat were pasturing about the dale, & moreover a long line of smoke was going up straight into the windless heavens from the midst of a ring of little round houses built of turfs, and thatched with reed. And beyond that, toward an eastward-lying bight of the dale, they could see what looked like to a doom-ring of big stones, though there were no rocky places in that land. About the cooking-fire amidst of the houses, and here & there otherwhere, they saw, standing or going to and fro, huge figures of men and women, with children playing about betwixt them.

THEY stood and gazed down at it for a minute or two, & though all were at peace there, yet to Walter, at least, it seemed strange & awful. He spake softly, as though he would not have his voice reach those men, though they were, forsooth, out of ear-shot of anything save a shout: Are these then the children of the Bear? What shall we do now?

She said: Yea, of the Bear they be, though there be other folks of them far & far away to the northward & eastward, near to the borders of the sea. And as to what we shall do, let us go down at once, and peacefully. Indeed, by now there will be no escape from them; for lo you! they have seen us.

FORSOOTH, some three or four of the big men had turned them toward the bent whereon stood the twain, & were hailing them in huge, rough voices, wherein, howsoever, seemed to be no anger or threat. So the Maid took Walter by the hand,

and thus they went down quietly, and the Bear-folk, seeing them, stood all together, facing them, to abide their coming. Walter saw of them, that though they were very tall and bigly made, they were not so far above the stature of men as to be marvels. The carles were long-haired, and shaggy of beard, and their hair all red or tawny; their skins, where their naked flesh showed, were burned brown with sun & weather, but to a fair and pleasant brown, nought like to blacka-moors. The queans were comely & well-eyed; nor was there anything of fierce or evil-looking about either the carles or the queans, but somewhat grave and solemn of aspect were they. Clad were they all, saving the young men-children, but somewhat scantily, and in nought save sheep-skins or deer-skins.

For weapons they saw amongst them clubs, & spears headed with bone or flint, and ugly axes of big flints set in wooden handles; nor was there, as far as they could see, either now or afterward, any bow amongst them. But some of the young men seemed to have slings done about their shoulders.

NOW when they were come but three fathom from them, the Maid lifted up her voice, and spake clearly and sweetly: Hail, ye folk of the Bears! we have come amongst you, & that for your good and not for your hurt: wherefore we would know if we be welcome.

THERE was an old man who stood foremost in the midst, clad in a mantle of deer-skins worked very goodly, and with a gold ring on his arm, and a chaplet of blue stones on his head, and he spake: Little are ye, but so goodly, that if ye were but bigger, we should deem that ye were come from the

Gods' House. Yet have I heard, that how mighty soever may the Gods be, & chiefly our God, they be at whiles nought so bigly made as we of the Bears. How this may be, I wot not. But if ye be not of the Gods or their kindred, then are ye mere aliens; & we know not what to do with aliens, save we meet them in battle, or give them to the God, or save we make them children of the Bear. But yet again, ye may be messengers of some folk who would bind friendship and alliance with us: in which case ye shall at the least depart in peace, and whiles ye are with us shall be our guests in all good cheer. Now, therefore, we bid you declare the matter unto us.

Then spake the Maid: Father, it were easy for us to declare what we be unto you here present. But, meseemeth, ye who be gathered round the fire here this evening are less than the whole tale of the children of the Bear.

So it is, Maiden, said the elder, that many more children hath the Bear.

This then we bid you, said the Maid, that ye send the tokens round & gather your people to you, and when they be assembled in the Doomring, then shall we put our errand before you; and according to that, shall ye deal with us.

Thou hast spoken well, said the elder; and even so had we bidden you ourselves. Tomorrow, before noon, shall ye stand in the Doomring in this Dale, & speak with the children of the Bear.

HEREWITH he turned to his own folk & called out something, whereof those twain knew not the meaning; & there came to him, one after another, six young men, unto each of whom he gave a thing from out his pouch, but what it was Walter might not see, save that it was little and of small account: to each, also, he spake a word or two, & straight they set off running, one after the other, turning toward the bent which was over against that whereby the twain had come into the Dale, and were soon out of sight in the gathering dusk.

THEN the elder turned him again to Walter and the Maid, & spake: Man and woman, whatsoever ye may be, or whatsoever may abide you to-morrow, to-night, ye are welcome guests to us; so we bid you come eat and drink at our fire.

SO they sat all together upon the grass round about the embers of the fire, and ate curds and cheese, and drank milk in abundance; & as the night grew on them they quickened the fire, that they might have light. This wild folk talked merrily amongst themselves, with laughter enough & friendly jests, but to the new-comers they were few-spoken, though, as the twain deemed, for no enmity that they bore them. But this found Walter, that the younger ones, both men and women, seemed to find it a hard matter to keep their eyes off them; and seemed, withal, to gaze on them with somewhat of doubt, or, it might be, of fear.

SO when the night was wearing a little, the elder arose and bade the twain to come with him, and led them to a small house or booth, which was amidmost of all, and somewhat bigger than the others, and he did them to wit that they should rest there that night, & bade them sleep in peace and without fear till the morrow. So they entered, and found beds thereon of heather and ling, and they laid them down sweetly, like brother and sister, when they had kissed each other. But they noted that four brisk men lay without the booth, & across the door, with their weapons beside them, so that they must needs look upon themselves as captives.

Then Walter might not refrain him, but spake: Sweet and dear friend, I have come a long way from the quay at Langton, and the vision of the Dwarf, the Maid, and the Lady; and for this kiss wherewith I have kissed thee e'en now, & the kindness of thine eyes, it was worth the time & the travail. But to-morrow, meseemeth, I shall go no further in this world, though my journey be far longer than from Langton hither. And now may God and All Hallows keep thee amongst this wild folk, whenas I shall be gone from thee.

She laughed low and sweetly, & said: Dear friend, dost thou speak to me thus mournfully to move me to love thee better? Then is thy labour lost; for no better may I love thee than now I do; and that is with mine whole heart. But keep a good courage, I bid thee; for we be not sundered yet, nor shall we be. Nor do I deem that we shall die here, or to-morrow; but many years hence, after we have known all the sweetness of life. Meanwhile, I bid thee good night, fair friend!

SO Walter laid him down & fell asleep, & knew no more till he awoke in bright daylight with the Maid standing over him. She was fresh from the water, for she had been to the river to bathe her, and the sun through the open door fell streaming on her feet close to Walter's pillow. He turned about & cast his arm about them, & caressed them, while she stood smiling upon him; then he arose and looked on her, and said: How thou art fair and bright this morning! And yet ... and yet ... were it not well that thou do off thee all this faded and drooping bravery of leaves and blossoms, that maketh thee look like to a jongleur's damsel on a morrow of Mayday?

And he gazed ruefully on her.

She laughed on him merrily, and said: Yea, & belike these others think no better of my attire, or not much better; for yonder they are gathering small wood for the burnt-offering; which, forsooth, shall be thou and I, unless I better it all by means of the wisdom I learned of the old woman, and perfected betwixt the stripes of my Mistress, whom a little while ago thou lovedst somewhat.

AND as she spake her eyes sparkled, her cheek flushed, and her limbs and her feet seemed as if they could scarce refrain from dancing for joy. Then Walter knit his brow, and for a moment a thought half-framed was in his mind. Is it so, that she will bewray me and live without me? and he cast his eyes on to the ground. But she said: Look up, & into mine eyes, friend, and see if there be in them any falseness toward thee! For I know thy thought; I know thy thought. Dost thou not see that my joy and gladness is for the love of thee, & the thought of the rest from trouble that is at hand?

He looked up, & his eyes met the eyes of her love, and he would have cast his arms about her; but she drew aback and said: Nay, thou must refrain thee awhile, dear friend, lest these folk cast eyes on us, and deem us over lover-like for what I am to bid them deem me. Abide a while, and then shall all be in me according to thy will. But now I must tell thee that it is not very far from noon, and that the Bears are streaming into the Dale, and already there is an host of men at the Doom-ring, &, as I said, the bale for the burnt-offering is well-nigh dight, whether it be for us, or for some other creature. And now I have to bid thee this, and it will be a thing easy for thee to do, to wit, that thou look as if thou wert of the race of the Gods, and not to blench, or show sign of blenching, whatever betide: to yea-say both my yea-say & my nay-say: and lastly this, which is the only hard thing for thee (but thou hast already done it before somewhat), to look upon me with no masterful eyes of love, nor as if thou wert at once praying me & commanding me; rather thou shalt so demean thee as if thou wert my man all simply, and nowise my master.

O friend beloved, said Walter, here at least art thou the master, and I will do all thy bidding, in certain hope of this, that either we shall live together or die together.

UT as they spoke, in came the elder, & with him a young maiden, bearing with them their breakfast of curds and cream and strawberries, and he bade them eat. So they ate, and were not unmerry; and the while of their eating the elder talked with them soberly, but not hardly, or with any seeming enmity: & ever his talk gat on to the drought, which was now burning up the down-pastures; & how the grass in the watered dales, which was no wide spread of land, would not hold out much longer unless the God sent them rain. And Walter noted that those two, the elder and the Maid, eyed each other curiously amidst of this talk; the elder intent on what she might say, & if she gave heed to his words; while on her side the Maid answered his speech graciously and pleasantly, but said little that was of any import: nor would she have him fix her eyes, which wandered lightly from this thing to that; nor would her lips grow stern and stable, but ever smiled in answer to the light of her eyes, as she sat there with her face as the very face of the gladness of the summer day.

T last the old man said: My child⁄
ren, ye shall now come with me unto
the Doom⁄ring of our folk, the
Bears of the Southern Dales, and
deliver to them your errand; and I
beseech you to have pity upon your
own bodies, as I have pity on them; on thine especially,
Maiden, so fair and bright a creature as thou art; for so
it is, that if ye deal us out light & lying words after the
manner of dastards, ye shall miss the worship & glory
of wending away amidst of the flames, a gift to the
God and a hope to the people, and shall be passed by
the rods of the folk, until ye faint & fail amongst them,
& then shall ye be thrust down into the flow at the
Dale's End, & a stone⁄laden hurdle cast upon you,
that we may thenceforth forget your folly.

The Maid now looked full into his eyes, and
Walter deemed that the old man shrank before her; but
she said: Thou art old and wise, O great man of the
Bears, yet nought I need to learn of thee. Now lead us
on our way to the Stead of the Errands.

SO the elder brought them along to the Doom⁄
ring at the eastern end of the Dale; and it was
now all peopled with those huge men, weapon⁄
ed after their fashion, and standing up, so that the grey
stones thereof but showed a little over their heads. But
amidmost of the said Ring was a big stone, fashioned
as a chair, whereon sat a very old man, long⁄hoary and
white⁄bearded, & on either side of him stood a great⁄
limbed woman clad in war⁄gear, holding, each of

them, a long spear, and with a flint-bladed knife in the girdle; and there were no other women in all the Mote.

THEN the elder led those twain into the midst of the Mote, and there bade them go up on to a wide, flat-topped stone, six feet above the ground, just over against the ancient chief-tain; and they mounted it by a rough stair, & stood there before that folk; Walter in his array of the out-ward world, which had been fair enough, of crimson cloth and silk, & white linen, but was now travel-stained and worn; & the Maid with nought upon her, save the smock wherein she had fled from the Golden House of the Wood beyond the World, decked with the faded flowers which she had wreathed about her yesterday. Nevertheless, so it was, that those big men eyed her intently, and with somewhat of worship.

NOW did Walter, according to her bidding, sink down on his knees beside her, & drawing his sword, hold it before him, as if to keep all interlopers aloof from the Maid. And there was silence in the Mote, & all eyes were fixed on those twain.

AT last the old chief arose and spake: Ye men, here are come a man and a woman, we know not whence; whereas they have given word to our folk who first met them, that they would tell their errand to none save the Mote of the People; which it was their due to do, if they were minded to risk it. For either they be aliens without an errand hither, save, it may be, to beguile us, in which case they shall presently die an evil death; or they have come amongst us that we may give them to the God with flint-edge and fire; or they have a message to us from some folk or other, on the issue of which lieth life or death. Now shall ye hear what they have to say concerning themselves and their faring hither. But, meseemeth, it shall be the woman who is the chief and hath the word in her mouth; for, lo you! the man kneeleth at her feet, as one who would serve and worship her. Speak out then, woman, and let our warriors hear thee.

THEN the Maid lifted up her voice, & spake out clear and shrilling, like to a flute of the best of the minstrels: Ye men of the Children of the Bear, I would ask you a question, and let the chieftain who sitteth before me answer it.

The old man nodded his head, and she went on: Tell me, Children of the Bear, how long a time is worn since ye saw the God of your worship made manifest in the body of a woman?

Said the elder: Many winters have worn since my father's father was a child, & saw the very God in the bodily form of a woman.

Then she said again: Did ye rejoice at her coming, and would ye rejoice if once more she came amongst you?

Yea, said the old chieftain, for she gave us gifts, and learned us lore, and came to us in no terrible shape, but as a young woman as goodly as thou.

Then said the Maid: Now, then, is the day of your gladness come; for the old body is dead, & I am the new body of your God, come amongst you for your welfare.

Then fell a great silence on the Mote, till the old man spake and said: What shall I say and live? For if thou be verily the God, and I threaten thee, wilt thou not destroy me? But thou hast spoken a great word with a sweet mouth, & hast taken the burden of blood on thy lily hands; and if the Children of the Bear be befooled of light liars, how shall they put the shame off them? Therefore I say, show to us a token; and if thou be the God, this shall be easy to thee; & if thou show it not, then is thy falsehood manifest, & thou shalt dree the weird. For we shall deliver thee into the hands of these women here, who shall thrust thee down into the flow which is hereby, after they have wearied themselves with whipping thee. But thy man that kneeleth at thy feet shall we give to the true God, and he shall go to her by the road of the flint and the fire. Hast thou heard? Then give to us the sign and the token.

SHE changed countenance no whit at his word; but her eyes were the brighter, and her cheek the fresher; and her feet moved a little, as if they were growing glad before the dance; & she looked out over the Mote, and spake in her clear voice: Old man, thou needest not to fear for thy words. Forsooth it is not me whom thou threatenest with stripes and a foul death, but some light fool and liar, who is not here. Now hearken! I wot well that ye would have somewhat of me, to wit, that I should send you rain to end this drought, which otherwise seemeth like to lie long upon you: but this rain, I must go into the mountains of the south to fetch it you; therefore shall certain of your warriors bring me on my way, with this my man, up to the great pass of the said mountains, and we shall set out thitherward this very day.

She was silent a while, & all looked on her, but none spake or moved, so that they seemed as images of stone amongst the stones.

Then she spake again and said: Some would say, men of the Bear, that this were a sign and a token great enough; but I know you, and how stubborn & perverse of heart ye be; and how that the gift not yet within your hand is no gift to you; and the wonder ye see not, your hearts trow not. Therefore look ye upon me as here I stand, I who have come from the fairer country and the green-wood of the lands, and see if I bear not the summer with me, and the heart that maketh increase and the hand that giveth.

LO then! as she spake, the faded flowers that hung about her gathered life and grew fresh again; the woodbine round her neck & her sleek shoulders knit itself together and embraced her freshly, and cast its scent about her face. The lilies that girded her loins lifted up their heads, and the gold of their tassels fell upon her; the eyebright grew clean blue again upon her smock; the eglantine found its blooms again, and then began to shed the leaves thereof upon her feet; the meadow-sweet wreathed amongst it made clear the sweetness of her legs, & the mouse-ear studded her raiment as with gems. There she stood amidst of the blossoms, like a great orient pearl against the fretwork of the goldsmiths, and the breeze that came up the valley from behind bore the sweetness of her fragrance all over the Man-mote.

THEN, indeed, the Bears stood up, and shouted and cried, and smote on their shields, & tossed their spears aloft. Then the elder rose from his seat, & came up humbly to where she stood, and prayed her to say what she would have done; while the others drew about in knots, but durst not come very nigh to her. She answered the ancient chief, and said, that she would depart presently toward the mountains, whereby she might send them the rain which they lacked, and that thence she would away to the southward for a while; but that they should hear of her, or, it might be, see her, before they who were now of middle age should be gone to their fathers.

Then the old man besought her that they might make her a litter of fragrant green boughs, and so bear her away toward the mountain pass amidst a triumph of the whole folk. But she leapt lightly down from the stone, and walked to and fro on the greensward, while it seemed of her that her feet scarce touched the grass; & she spake to the ancient chief where he still kneeled in worship of her, & said: Nay; deemest thou of me that I need bearing by men's hands, or that I shall tire at all when I am doing my will, and I, the very heart of the year's increase? So it is, that the going of my feet over your pastures shall make them to thrive, both this year and the coming years: surely will I go afoot.

S O they worshipped her the more, and blessed her; and then first of all they brought meat, the daintiest they might, both for her and for Walter. But they would not look on the Maid whiles she ate, or suffer Walter to behold her the while. Afterwards, when they had eaten, some twenty men, weaponed after their fashion, made them ready to wend with the Maiden up into the mountains, and anon they set out thitherward all together. Howbeit, the huge men held them ever somewhat aloof from the Maid; & when they came to the resting-place for that night, where was no house, for it was up amongst the foot-hills before the mountains, then it was a wonder to see how carefully they built up a sleeping-place for her,

& tilted it over with their skin-cloaks, and how they watched night-long about her. But Walter they let sleep peacefully on the grass, a little way aloof from the watchers round the Maid.

CHAPTER XXIX · WALTER STRAYS IN THE PASS & IS SUNDERED FROM THE MAID

ORNING came, & they arose and went on their ways, and went all day till the sun was nigh set, and they were come up into the very pass; & in the jaws thereof was an earthen howe. There the Maid bade them stay, & she went up on to the howe, & stood there and spake to them, and said: O men of the Bear, I give you thanks for your following, and I bless you, and promise you the increase of the earth. But now ye shall turn aback, and leave me to go my ways; and my man with the iron sword shall follow me. Now, maybe, I shall come amongst the Bear-folk again before long, and yet again, & learn them wisdom; but for this time it is enough. And I shall tell you that ye were best to hasten home straightway to your houses in the down-land dales, for the weather which I have bidden for you is even now coming forth from the forge of storms in the heart of the mountains. Now this last word I give you, that times are changed since I wore the last shape of God that ye have seen, wherefore a change I command you. If so be aliens come amongst you, I will not that ye send them to me by the flint &

the fire; rather, unless they be baleful unto you, & worthy of an evil death, ye shall suffer them to abide with you; ye shall make them become children of the Bears, if they be goodly enough & worthy, & they shall be my children as ye be; otherwise, if they be ill-favoured and weakling, let them live & be thralls to you, but not join with you, man to woman. Now depart ye with my blessing.

HEREWITH she came down from the mound, and went her ways up the pass so lightly, that it was to Walter, standing amongst the Bears, as if she had vanished away. But the men of that folk abode standing and worshipping their God for a little while, and that while he durst not sunder him from their company. But when they had blessed him and gone on their way backward, he betook him in haste to following the Maid, thinking to find her abiding him in some nook of the pass.

HOWSOEVER, it was now twilight or more, &, for all his haste, dark night overtook him, so that perforce he was stayed amidst the tangle of the mountain ways. And, moreover, ere the night was grown old, the weather came upon him on the back of a great south wind, so that the mountain nooks rattled and roared, & there was the rain & the hail, with thunder and lightning, monstrous and terrible, and all the huge array of a summer storm. So he was driven at last to crouch under a big rock and abide the day.

BUT not so were his troubles at an end. For under the said rock he fell asleep, and when he awoke it was day indeed; but as to the pass, the way thereby was blind with the driving rain and the lowering lift; so that, though he struggled as

142

well as he might against the storm & the tangle, he made but little way.

AND now once more the thought came on him, that the Maid was of the fays, or of some race even mightier; and it came on him now not as erst, with half fear and whole desire, but with a bitter oppression of dread, of loss and misery; so that he began to fear that she had but won his love to leave him and forget him for a newcomer, after the wont of fay-women, as old tales tell.

TWO days he battled thus with storm & blindness, & wanhope of his life; for he was growing weak & fordone. But the third morning the storm abated, though the rain yet fell heavily, and he could see his way somewhat as well as feel it: withal he found that now his path was leading him downwards. As it grew dusk, he came down into a grassy valley with a stream running through it to the south ward, and the rain was now but little, coming down but in dashes from time to time. So he crept down to the stream-side, & lay amongst the bushes there; & said to himself, that on the morrow he would get him victual, so that he might live to seek his Maiden through the wide world. He was of somewhat better heart: but now that he was laid quiet, & had no more for that present to trouble him about the way, the anguish of his loss fell upon him the keener, and he might not refrain him from lamenting his dear Maiden aloud, as one who deemed himself in the empty wilderness: & thus he lamented for her sweetness and her loveliness, and the kindness of her voice & her speech, & her mirth. Then he fell to crying out concerning the beauty of her shaping, praising the parts of her body, as her face, and her hands, and her shoulders, and her feet, and cursing the evil fate which had sundered him from the friendliness of her, and the peerless fashion of her.

CHAPTER XXX · NOW THEY MEET AGAIN

COMPLAINING thus-wise, he fell asleep from sheer weariness, & when he awoke it was broad day, calm and bright and cloudless, with the scent of the earth refreshed going up into the heavens, and the birds singing sweetly in the bushes about him: for the dale whereunto he was now come was a fair and lovely place amidst the shelving slopes of the mountains, a paradise of the wilderness, and nought but pleasant and sweet things were to be seen there, now that the morn was so clear and sunny.

HE arose and looked about him, & saw where, a hundred yards aloof, was a thicket of small wood, as thorn & elder & whitebeam, all wreathed about with the bines of wayfaring tree; it hid a bight of the stream, which turned round about it, and betwixt it and Walter was the grass short and thick, and sweet, & all beset with flowers; and he said to himself that it was even such a place as wherein the angels were leading the Blessed in the great painted paradise in the choir of the big church at Langton on Holm. But lo! as he looked he cried aloud for joy, for forth from the thicket on to the flowery grass came one like to an angel from out of the said picture, white-clad and bare-foot, sweet of flesh, with bright eyes and ruddy cheeks; for it was the Maid herself. So he ran to her, and she abode him, holding forth kind hands to him, and smiling, while she wept for joy of the meeting. He threw himself upon her, and spared not to kiss her, her cheeks and her mouth, & her arms and her shoulders, & wheresoever she would suffer it. Till at last she drew aback a little, laughing on him for love, and said: Forbear now, friend, for it is enough for this time, and tell me how thou hast sped.

Ill, ill, said he.

What ails thee? she said.

Hunger, he said, and longing for thee.

Well, she said, me thou hast; there is one ill quenched; take my hand, & we will see to the other one.

So he took her hand, and to hold it seemed to him sweet beyond measure. But he looked up, and saw a little blue smoke going up into the air from beyond the thicket; and he laughed, for he was weak with hunger, & he said: Who is at the cooking yonder?

Thou shalt see, she said; and led him therewith into the said thicket & through it, and lo! a fair little grassy place, full of flowers, betwixt the bushes and the bight of the stream; and on the little sandy ere, just off the greensward, was a fire of sticks, & beside it two trouts lying, fat and red-flecked.

Here is the breakfast, said she; when it was time to wash the night off me e'en now, I went down the strand here into the rippling shallow, & saw the bank below it, where the water draws together yonder, & deepens, that it seemed like to hold fish; and, whereas I looked to meet thee presently, I groped the bank for them, going softly; and lo thou! Help me now, that we cook them.

SO they roasted them on the red embers, and fell to and ate well, both of them, and drank of the water of the stream out of each other's hollow hands; and that feast seemed glorious to them, such gladness went with it.

BUT when they were done with their meat, Walter said to the Maid:

And how didst thou know that thou shouldst see me presently?

She said, looking on him wistfully: This needed no wizardry. I lay not so far from thee last night, but that I heard thy voice and knew it.

Said he, Why didst thou not come to me then, since thou heardest me bemoaning thee?

She cast her eyes down, and plucked at the flowers and grass, and said: It was dear to hear thee praising me; I knew not before that I was so sore desired, or that thou hadst taken such note of my body, & found it so dear.

Then she reddened sorely, and said: I knew not that aught of me had such beauty as thou didst bewail.

And she wept for joy. Then she looked on him and smiled, & said: Wilt thou have the very truth of it? I went close up to thee, and stood there hidden by the bushes and the night. And amidst thy bewailing, I knew that thou wouldst soon fall asleep, and in sooth I out-waked thee.

THEN was she silent again; and he spake not, but looked on her shyly; and she said, reddening yet more: Furthermore, I must needs tell thee that I feared to go to thee in the dark

146

night, and my heart so yearning towards thee.

And she hung her head adown; but he said: Is it so indeed, that thou fearest me? Then doth that make me afraid . . . afraid of thy nay-say. For I was going to entreat thee, & say to thee: Beloved, we have now gone through many troubles; let us now take a good reward at once, & wed together, here amidst this sweet and pleasant house of the mountains, ere we go further on our way; if indeed we go further at all. For where shall we find any place sweeter or happier than this?

BUT she sprang up to her feet, and stood there trembling before him, because of her love; and she said: Beloved, I have deemed that it were good for us to go seek mankind as they live in the world, and to live amongst them. And as for me, I will tell thee the sooth, to wit, that I long for this sorely. For I feel afraid in the wilderness, and as if I needed help and protection against my Mistress, though she be dead; and I need the comfort of many people, and the throngs of the cities. I cannot forget her: it was but last night that I dreamed (I suppose as the dawn grew a-cold) that I was yet under her hand, and she was stripping me for the torment; so that I woke up panting and crying out. I pray thee be not angry with me for telling thee of my desires; for if thou wouldst not have it so, then here will I abide with thee as thy mate, and strive to gather courage.

HE rose up and kissed her face, & said: Nay, I had in sooth no mind to abide here for ever; I meant but that we should feast a while here, and then depart: sooth it is, that if thou dreadest the wilderness, somewhat I dread the city.

She turned pale, & said: Thou shalt have thy will,

my friend, if it must be so. But bethink thee! we be not yet at our journey's end, and may have many things and much strife to endure, before we be at peace and in welfare. Now shall I tell thee . . . did I not before? . . . that while I am a maid untouched, my wisdom, and somedeal of might, abideth with me, and only so long. Therefore I entreat thee, let us go now, side by side, out of this fair valley, even as we are, so that my wisdom and might may help thee at need. For, my friend, I would not that our lives be short, so much of joy as hath now come into them.

Yea, beloved, he said, let us on straightway then, and shorten the while that sundereth us.

Love, she said, thou shalt pardon me one time for all. But this is to be said, that I know somewhat of the haps that lie a little way ahead of us; partly by my lore, and partly by what I learned of this land of the wild folk whiles thou wert lying asleep that morning.

SO they left that pleasant place by the water, and came into the open valley, and went their ways through the pass; and it soon became stony again, as they mounted the bent which went up from out the dale. And when they came to the brow of the said bent, they had a sight of the open country lying fair and joyous in the sunshine, & amidst of it, against the blue hills, the walls and towers of a great city.

Then said the Maid: O, dear friend, lo you! is not that our abode that lieth yonder, and is so beauteous? Dwell not our friends there, and our protection against uncouth wights, and mere evil things in guileful shapes? O city, I bid thee hail!

But Walter looked on her, and smiled somewhat; and said: I rejoice in thy joy. But there be evil things in yonder city also, though they be not fays nor devils, or it is like to no city that I wot of. And in every city shall foes grow up to us without rhyme or reason, and life therein shall be tangled unto us.

Yea, she said; but in the wilderness amongst the devils, what was to be done by manly might or valiancy? There hadst thou to fall back upon the guile and wizardry which I had filched from my very foes. But when we come down yonder, then shall thy valiancy prevail to cleave the tangle for us. Or at the least, it shall leave a tale of thee behind, & I shall worship thee.

He laughed, and his face grew brighter: Mastery mows the meadow, quoth he, and one man is of little might against many. But I promise thee I shall not be slothful before thee.

CHAPTER XXXI ⁄ THEY COME UPON NEW FOLK

ITH that they went down from the bent again, and came to where the pass narrowed so much, that they went betwixt a steep wall of rock on either side; but after an hour's going, the said wall gave back suddenly, and, or they were ware almost, they came on another dale like to that which they had left, but not so fair, though it was grassy and well watered, & not so big either. But here indeed befell a change to them; for lo! tents and pavilions pitched in the said valley, and amidst of it a throng of men, mostly

weaponed, and with horses ready saddled at hand. So they stayed their feet, & Walter's heart failed him, for he said to himself: Who wotteth what these men may be, save that they be aliens? It is most like that we shall be taken as thralls; and then, at the best, we shall be sundered; & that is all one with the worst.

BUT the Maid, when she saw the horses, & the gay tents, and the pennons fluttering, & the glitter of spears, and gleaming of white armour, smote her palms together for joy, and cried out: Here now are come the folk of the city for our welcoming, and fair and lovely are they, & of many things shall they be thinking, & a many things shall they do, and we shall be partakers thereof. Come then, and let us meet them, fair friend!

But Walter said: Alas! thou knowest not: would that we might flee! But now is it over late; so put we a good face on it, and go to them quietly, as erewhile we did in the Bear-country.

SO did they; and there sundered six from the men-at-arms and came to those twain, and made humble obeisance to Walter, but spake no word. Then they made as they would lead them to the others, and the twain went with them wondering, and came into the ring of men-at-arms, & stood before an old hoar knight, armed all, save his head, with most goodly armour, and he also bowed before Walter, but spake no word. Then they took them to the master pavilion, and made signs to them to sit, and they brought them dainty meat and good wine. And the while of their eating arose up a stir about them; and when they were done with their meat, the ancient knight came to them, still bowing in courteous wise, and did them to wit by signs that they should depart: & when they were without, they saw all the other tents struck, and men beginning to busy them with striking the pavilion, and the others mounted and ranked in good order for the road; & there were two horse-litters before them, wherein they were bidden to mount, Walter in one, and the Maid in the other, and no otherwise might they do. Then presently was a horn blown, & all took to the road together; and Walter saw betwixt the curtains of the litter that men-at-arms rode on either side of him, albeit they had left him his sword by his side.

SO they went down the mountain-passes, and before sunset were gotten into the plain; but they made no stay for night-fall, save to eat a morsel and drink a draught, going through the night as men who knew their way well. As they went, Walter wondered what would betide, and if peradventure they also would be for offering them up to their Gods; whereas they were aliens for certain, & belike also Saracens. Moreover there was a cold fear at his heart that he should be sundered from the Maid, whereas their masters now were mighty men of war, holding in their hands that which all men desire, to wit, the manifest beauty of a woman. Yet he strove to think the best of it that he might. And so at last, when the night was far spent, and dawn was at hand, they stayed at a great & mighty gate in a huge wall. There they blew loudly on the horn thrice, & thereafter the gates were opened, & they all passed through into a street, which seemed to Walter in the glimmer to be both great & goodly amongst the abodes of men. Then it was but a little ere they came into a square, wide-spreading, one side whereof Walter took to be the front of a most goodly house. There the doors of the court opened to them or ever the horn might blow, though, forsooth, blow it did loudly three times; all they entered therein, and men came to Walter and signed to him to alight. So did he, & would have tarried to look about for the Maid, but they suffered it not, but led him up a huge stair into a chamber, very great, and but dimly lighted because of its greatness. Then they brought him to a bed dight as fair as might be, & made signs to him to strip and lie therein. Perforce he did so, and then they bore away his raiment, & left him lying there. So he lay there quietly, deeming it no avail for him, a mother‑naked man, to seek escape thence; but it was long ere he might sleep, because of his trouble of mind. At last, pure weariness got the better of his hopes and fears, and he fell into slumber just as the dawn was passing into day.

CHAPTER XXXII ‑ OF THE NEW KING OF THE CITY AND LAND OF STARK‑ WALL

HEN he awoke again the sun was shining brightly into that chamber, and he looked, and beheld that it was peerless of beauty & riches, amongst all that he had ever seen: the ceiling done with gold and over‑sea blue; the walls hung with arras of the fairest, though he might not tell what was the history done therein. The chairs and stools were of carven work well be‑painted,

& amidmost was a great ivory chair under a cloth of estate, of bawdekin of gold and green, much be-pearled; & all the floor was of fine work alexandrine.

HE looked on all this, wondering what had befallen him, when lo! there came folk into the chamber, to wit, two serving-men well-bedight, and three old men clad in rich gowns of silk. These came to him and (still by signs, without speech) bade him arise and come with them; and when he bade them look to it that he was naked, and laughed doubtfully, they neither laughed in answer, nor offered him any raiment, but still would have him arise, and he did so perforce. They brought him with them out of the chamber, and through certain passages pillared and goodly, till they came to a bath as fair as any might be; and there the serving-men washed him carefully & tenderly, the old men looking on the while. When it was done, still they offered not to clothe him, but led him out, & through the passages again, back to the chamber. Only this time he must pass between a double hedge of men, some weaponed, some in peaceful array, but all clad gloriously, & full chieftain-like of aspect, either for valiancy or wisdom.

IN the chamber itself was now a concourse of men, of great estate by deeming of their array; but all these were standing orderly in a ring about the ivory chair aforesaid. Now said Walter to himself: Surely all this looks toward the knife and the altar for me; but he kept a stout countenance despite of all.

SO they led him up to the ivory chair, & he beheld on either side thereof a bench, & on each was laid a set of raiment from the shirt upwards; but there was much diversity betwixt these arrays. For one was all of robes of peace, glorious & begemmed, unmeet for any save a great king; while the other was war-weed, seemly, well-fashioned, but little adorned; nay rather, worn and bestained with weather, and the pelting of the spear-storm.

NOW those old men signed to Walter to take which of those raiments he would, and do it on. He looked to the right and the left, and when he had looked on the war-gear, the heart arose in him, and he called to mind the array of the Goldings in the forefront of battle, and he made one step toward the weapons, and laid his hand thereon. Then ran a glad murmur through that concourse, and the old men drew up to him smiling & joyous, and helped him to do them on; & as he took up the helm, he noted that over its broad brown iron sat a golden crown.

SO when he was clad & weaponed, girt with a sword, & a steel axe in his hand, the elders showed him to the ivory throne, and he laid the axe on the arm of the chair, and drew forth the sword from the scabbard, and sat him down, and laid the ancient blade across his knees; then he looked about on those great men, & spake: How long shall we speak no word to each other, or is it so that God hath stricken you dumb?

THEN all they cried out with one voice: All hail to the King, the King of Battle!

Spake Walter: If I be king, will ye do my will as I bid you?

Answered the elder: Nought have we will to do, lord, save as thou biddest.

154

Said Walter: Thou then, wilt thou answer a question in all truth?

Yea, lord, said the elder, if I may live afterward.

Then said Walter: The woman that came with me into your Camp of the Mountain, what hath befallen her?

The elder answered: Nought hath befallen her, either of good or evil, save that she hath slept and eaten and bathed her. What, then, is the King's pleasure concerning her?

That ye bring her hither to me straightway, said Walter.

Yea, said the elder; & in what guise shall we bring her hither? shall she be arrayed as a servant, or a great lady?

Then Walter pondered a while, and spake at last: Ask her what is her will herein, and as she will have it, so let it be. But set ye another chair beside mine, & lead her thereto. Thou wise old man, send one or two to bring her in hither, but abide thou, for I have a question or two to ask of thee yet. And ye, lords, abide here the coming of my she-fellow, if it weary you not.

SO the elder spake to three of the most honourable of the lords, & they went their ways to bring in the Maid.

CHAPTER XXXIII · CONCERNING THE FASHION OF KING-MAKING IN STARK-WALL

EANWHILE the King spake to the elder, & said: Now tell me where-of I am become king, and what is the fashion and cause of the king-making; for wondrous it is to me, whereas I am but an alien amidst of mighty men.

Lord, said the old man, thou art become king of a mighty city, which hath under it many other cities and wide lands, and havens by the sea-side, and which lacketh no wealth which men desire. Many wise men dwell therein, and of fools not more than in other lands. A valiant host shall follow thee to battle when needs must thou wend afield; an host not to be withstood, save by the ancient God-folk, if any of them were left upon the earth, as belike none are. And as to the name of our said city, it hight the City of the Stark-wall, or more shortly, Stark-wall. Now as to the fashion of our king-making: If our king dieth & leaveth an heir male, begotten of his body, then is he king after him; but if he die & leave no heir, then send we out a great lord, with knights and sergeants, to that pass of the mountain whereto ye came yesterday; & the first man that cometh unto them, they take & lead to the city, as they did with thee, lord. For we believe and trow that of old time our forefathers came down from the moun-tains by that same pass, poor and rude, but full of valiancy, before they conquered these lands, and builded the Stark-wall. But now furthermore, when we have gotten the said wanderer, & brought him home to our city, we behold him mother-naked, all the great men of us, both sages & warriors; then if we find him ill-fashioned and counterfeit of his body, we roll him in a great carpet till he dies; or whiles, if he be but a simple man, and without guile, we deliver him for thrall to some artificer amongst us, as a shoe-maker, a wright, or what not, & so forget him. But in either case we make as if no such man had come to us, and we send again the lord and his knights to watch the pass; for we say that such an one the Fathers of old time have not sent us. But again, when we have seen to the newcomer that he is well-fashioned of his body, all is not done; for we deem that never would the Fathers send us a dolt or a craven to be our king. Therefore we bid the naked one take to him which he will of these raiments, either the ancient armour, which now thou bearest, lord, or this golden raiment here; and if he take the war-gear, as thou takedst it, King, it is well; but if he take the raiment of peace, then hath he the choice either to be thrall of some goodman of the city, or to be proven how wise he may be, & so fare the narrow edge betwixt death and kingship; for if he fall short of his wisdom, then shall he die the death. Thus is thy question answered, King, and praise be to the Fathers that they have sent us one whom none may doubt, either for wisdom or valiancy.

HEN all they bowed before the King, & he spake again: What is that noise that I hear without, as if it were the rising of the sea on a sandy shore, when the south⁄west wind is blowing?

Then the elder opened his mouth to answer; but before he might get out the word, there was a stir without the chamber door, and the throng parted, and lo! amidst of them came the Maid, & she yet clad in nought save the white coat wherewith she had won through the wilderness, save that on her head was a garland of red roses, and her middle was wreathed with the same. Fresh & fair she was as the dawn of June; her face bright, red⁄lipped, and clear⁄eyed, and her cheeks flushed with hope and love. She went straight to Walter where he sat, and lightly put away with her hand the elder who would lead her to the ivory throne beside the King; but she knelt down before him, & laid her hand on his steel⁄clad knee, and said: O my lord, now I see that thou hast beguiled me, and that thou wert all along a king⁄born man coming home to thy realm. But so dear thou hast been to me; and so fair and clear, and so kind withal do thine eyes shine on me from under the grey war⁄helm, that I will beseech thee not to cast me out utterly, but suffer me to be thy servant & hand⁄maid for a while. Wilt thou not?

BUT the King stooped down to her and raised her up, & stood on his feet, and took her hands and kissed them, and set her down beside him, and said to her: Sweetheart, this is now thy place till the night cometh, even by my side.

So she sat down there meek and valiant, her hands laid in her lap, & her feet one over the other; while the King said: Lords, this is my beloved, & my spouse. Now, therefore, if ye will have me for King, ye must worship this one for Queen and Lady; or else suffer us both to go our ways in peace.

THEN all they that were in the chamber cried out aloud: The Queen, the Lady! The beloved of our lord! And this cry came from their hearts, & not their lips only; for as they looked on her, and the brightness of her beauty, they saw also the meekness of her demeanour, and the high heart of her, & they all fell to loving her. But the young men of them, their cheeks flushed as they beheld her, and their hearts went out to her, & they drew their swords & brandished them aloft, & cried out for her as men made suddenly drunk with love: The Queen, the Lady, the lovely one!

CHAPTER XXXV / OF THE KING OF STARK/WALL AND HIS QUEEN

UT while this betid, that murmur without, which is aforesaid, grew louder; & it smote on the King's ear, and he said again to the elder: Tell us now of that noise withoutward, what is it?

Said the elder: If thou, King, and the Queen, wilt but arise and stand in the window, and go forth into the hanging gallery thereof, then shall ye know at once what is this rumour, and therewithal shall ye see a sight meet to rejoice the heart of a king new come into kingship.

O the King arose & took the Maid by the hand, & went to the window and looked forth; and lo! the great square of the place all thronged with folk as thick as they could stand, and the more part of the carles with a weapon in hand, and many armed right gallantly. Then he went out into the gallery with his Queen, still holding her hand, and his lords & wise men stood behind him. Straightway then arose a cry, and a shout of joy & welcome that rent the very heavens, & the great place was all glittering and strange with the tossing up of spears & the brand/ishing of swords, & the stretching forth of hands.

UT the Maid spake softly to King Walter and said: Here then is the wilderness left behind a long way and here is warding and protection against the foes of our life and soul. O blessed be thou & thy valiant heart!

But Walter spake nothing, but stood as one in a

dream; & yet, if that might be, his longing toward her increased manifold.

BUT down below, amidst of the throng, stood two neighbours somewhat anigh to the window; and quoth one to the other: See thou! the new man in the ancient armour of the Battle of the Waters, bearing the sword that slew the foeman king on the Day of the Doubtful Onset! Surely this is a sign of good-luck to us all.

Yea, said the second, he beareth his armour well, and the eyes are bright in the head of him; but hast thou beheld well his she-fellow, and what the like of her is?

I see her, said the other, that she is a fair woman; yet somewhat worse clad than simply. She is in her smock, man, and were it not for the balusters I deem ye should see her barefoot. What is amiss with her?

Dost thou not see her, said the second neighbour, that she is not only a fair woman, but yet more, one of those lovely ones that draw the heart out of a man's body, one may scarce say for why? Surely Stark-wall hath cast a lucky net this time. And as to her raiment, I see of her that she is clad in white & wreathed with roses, but that the flesh of her is so wholly pure & sweet that it maketh all her attire but a part of her body, and halloweth it, so that it hath the semblance of gems. Alas, my friend! let us hope that this Queen will fare abroad unseldom amongst the people.

THUS, then, they spake; but after a while the King & his mate went back into the chamber, & he gave command that the women of the Queen should come and fetch her away, to attire her in royal array. And thither came the fairest of the honourable damsels, & were fain of being her waiting-women. Therewithal the King was unarmed, & dight most gloriously, but still be bore the Sword of the King's Slaying: and sithence were the King and the Queen brought into the great hall of the palace, and they met on the dais, & kissed before the lords and other folk that thronged the hall. There they ate a morsel and drank a cup together, while all beheld them; & then were they brought forth, & a white horse of the goodliest, well bedight, brought for each of them, and thereon they mounted, and went their ways together, by the lane which the huge throng made for them, to the great church, for the hallowing and the crowning; & they were led by one squire alone, and he unarmed; for such was the custom of Stark-wall when a new king should be hallowed: so came they to the great church (for that folk was not miscreant, so to say), and they entered it, they two alone, and went into the choir; & when they had stood there a little while wondering at their lot, they heard how the bells fell a-ringing tunefully over their heads; and then drew near the sound of many trumpets blowing together, and thereafter the voices of many folk singing; and then were the great doors thrown open, and the bishop and his priests came into the church with singing and minstrelsy, and thereafter came the whole throng of the folk, and presently the nave of the church was filled by it, as when the water follows the cutting of the dam, and fills up the dyke. Thereafter came the bishop & his mates into the choir, and came up to the King, and gave him and the Queen the kiss of peace. Then was mass sung gloriously; and thereafter was the King anointed & crowned, & great joy was made throughout the church. Afterwards they went back afoot to the palace, they two alone together, with none but the esquire going before to show them the way. And as they went, they passed close beside those two neighbours, whose talk has been told of afore, and the first one, he who had praised the King's war-array, spake and said: Truly, neighbour, thou art in the right of it; & now the Queen has been dight duly, and hath a crown on her head, and is clad in white samite done all over with pearls, I see her to be of exceeding goodliness; as goodly, maybe, as the Lord King.

Quoth the other: Unto me she seemeth as she did e'en now; she is clad in white, as then she was, and it is by reason of the pure and sweet flesh of her that the pearls shine out and glow, & by the holiness of her body is her rich attire hallowed; but, forsooth, it seemed to me as she went past as though paradise had come anigh to our city, and that all the air breathed of it. So I say, praise be to God and his Hallows who hath suffered her to dwell amongst us!

Said the first man: Forsooth, it is well; but knowest thou at all whence she cometh, and of what lineage she may be?

Nay, said the other, I wot not whence she is; but this I wot full surely, that when she goeth away, they whom she leadeth with her shall be well bestead. Again, of her lineage nought know I; but this I know, that they that come of her, to the twentieth generation, shall bless and praise the memory of her, & hallow her name little less than they hallow the name of the Mother of God.

S O spake those two; but the King and Queen came back to the palace, & sat among the lords and at the banquet which was held thereafter, and long was the time of their glory, till the night was far spent and all men must seek to their beds.

CHAPTER XXXVI ⁄ OF WALTER AND THE MAID IN THE DAYS OF THE KINGSHIP

L ONG it was, indeed, till the women, by the King's command, had brought the Maid to the King's chamber; and he met her, & took her by the shoulders and kissed her, and said: Art thou not weary, sweetheart? Doth not the city, and the thronging folk, and the watching eyes of the great ones . . . doth it not all lie heavy on thee, as it doth upon me?

She said: And where is the city now? is not this the wilderness again, and thou and I alone together therein?

He gazed at her eagerly, and she reddened, so that her eyes shone light amidst the darkness of the flush of her cheeks.

He spake trembling and softly, and said: Is it not in one matter better than the wilderness? is not the fear gone, yea, every whit thereof?

The dark flush had left her face, & she looked on him exceeding sweetly, and spoke steadily & clearly: Even so it is, beloved. Therewith she set her hand to the girdle that girt her loins, and did it off, and held it out toward him, and said: Here is the token; this is a maid's girdle, and the woman is ungirt.

So he took the girdle & her hand withal, & cast his arms about her: and amidst the sweetness of their love and their safety, & assured hope of many days of joy, they spake together of the hours when they feared the razor-edge betwixt guile & misery and death, and the sweeter yet it grew to them because of it; and many things she told him ere the dawn, of the evil days bygone, and the dealings of the Mistress with her, till the grey day stole into the chamber to make manifest her loveliness; which, forsooth, was better even than the deeming of that man amidst the throng whose heart had been so drawn towards her. So they rejoiced together in the new day.

BUT when the full day was, & Walter arose, he called his thanes & wise men to the council; & first he bade open the prison-doors, & feed the needy and clothe them, and make good cheer to all men, high and low, rich & unrich; and thereafter he took counsel with them on many matters, and they marvelled at his wisdom and the keenness of his wit; and so it was, that some were but half pleased thereat, whereas they saw that their will was like to give way before his in all matters. But the wiser of them rejoiced in him, and looked for good days while his life lasted.

NOW of the deeds that he did, & his joys and his griefs, the tale shall tell no more; nor of how he saw Langton again, and his dealings there.

In Stark-wall he dwelt, and reigned a King, well beloved of his folk, sorely feared of their foemen. Strife he had to deal with, at home and abroad; but therein he was not quelled, till he fell asleep fair and softly, when this world had no more of deeds for him to do. Nor may it be said that the needy lamented him; for no needy had he left in his own land. And few foes he left behind to hate him.

AS to the Maid, she so waxed in loveliness and kindness, that it was a year's joy for any to have cast eyes upon her in street or on field. All wizardry left her since the day of her wedding; yet of wit and wisdom she had enough left, and to spare; for she needed no going about, & no guile, any more than hard commands, to have her will done. So loved she was by all folk, forsooth, that it was a mere joy for any to go about her errands. To be short, she was the land's increase, and the city's safeguard, and the bliss of the folk.

SOMEWHAT, as the days passed, it mis-gave her that she had beguiled the Bear-folk to deem her their God; & she considered and thought how she might atone it.

So the second year after they had come to Stark-wall, she went with certain folk to the head of the pass that led down to the Bears; and there she stayed the men-at-arms, and went on further with a two score of husband-men whom she had redeemed from thralldom in Stark-wall; & when they were hard on the dales of the Bears, she left them there in a certain little dale, with their wains and horses, and seed-corn, & iron tools, & went down all bird-alone to the dwelling of those huge men, unguarded now by sorcery, and trusting in nought but her loveliness and kindness. Clad she was now, as when she fled from the Wood beyond the World, in a short white coat alone, with bare feet and naked arms; but the said coat was now embroidered with the imagery of blossoms in silk and gold, and gems, whereas now her wizardry had departed from her.

So she came to the Bears, and they knew her at once, and worshipped and blessed her, and feared her. But she told them that she had a gift for them, and was come to give it; and therewith she told them of the art of tillage, and bade them learn it; & when they asked her how they should do so, she told them of the men who were abiding them in the mountain dale, and bade the Bears take them for their brothers and sons of the ancient Fathers, and then they should be taught of them. This they behight her to do, and so she led them to where her freedmen lay, whom the Bears received with all joy and loving-kindness, & took them into their folk.

So they went back to their dales together; but the Maid went her ways back to her men-at-arms and the city of Stark-wall.

HEREAFTER she sent more gifts & messages to the Bears, but never again went herself to see them; for as good a face as she put on it that last time, yet her heart waxed cold with fear, and it almost seemed to her that her Mistress was alive again, and that she was escaping from her & plotting against her once more.

AS for the Bears, they throve and multiplied; till at last strife arose great & grim betwixt them & other peoples; for they had become mighty in battle: yea, once & again they met the host of Stark-wall in fight, & overthrew and were overthrown. But that was a long while after the Maid had passed away.

NOW of Walter and the Maid is no more to be told, saving that they begat between them goodly sons and fair daughters; whereof came a great lineage in Stark-wall; which lineage was so strong, & endured so long a while, that by then it had died out, folk had clean forgotten their ancient custom of king-making; so that after Walter of Langton there was never another king that came down to them poor & lonely from out of the Mountains of the Bears.

HERE ends the tale of the Wood beyond the World, made by William Morris, and printed by him at the Kelmscott Press, Upper Mall, Hammersmith. Finished the 30th day of May, 1894.